T0165527

JOB'S WAR

JOB'S WAR

CRACKER IRVIN

iUniverse, Inc.
Bloomington

Job's War

Copyright © 2012 by Cracker Irvin.

All rights reserved. No part of this book may be used or reproduced by any means, graphic, electronic, or mechanical, including photocopying, recording, taping or by any information storage retrieval system without the written permission of the publisher except in the case of brief quotations embodied in critical articles and reviews.

Certain characters in this work are historical figures, and certain events portrayed did take place. However, this is a work of fiction. All of the other characters, names, and events as well as all places, incidents, organizations, and dialogue in this novel are either the products of the author's imagination or are used fictitiously.

iUniverse books may be ordered through booksellers or by contacting:

iUniverse
1663 Liberty Drive
Bloomington, IN 47403
www.iuniverse.com
1-800-Authors (1-800-288-4677)

Because of the dynamic nature of the Internet, any web addresses or links contained in this book may have changed since publication and may no longer be valid. The views expressed in this work are solely those of the author and do not necessarily reflect the views of the publisher, and the publisher hereby disclaims any responsibility for them.

Any people depicted in stock imagery provided by Thinkstock are models, and such images are being used for illustrative purposes only.
Certain stock imagery © Thinkstock.

ISBN: 978-1-4759-5245-2 (sc)
ISBN: 978-1-4759-5246-9 (ebk)

Library of Congress Control Number: 2012918001

Printed in the United States of America

iUniverse rev. date: 10/26/2012

CONTENTS

ACKNOWLEDGEMENT

To (Buzzard) Larry Rackley and (Puddin') Leann Rackley.

Thanks for all you do!

FOREWORD

Shoot 'em up cowboys and Indians was a favorite past time growing up in East Texas. We loved to play the role of bloodthirsty, naked, screaming and bareback horse riding Indian with a Mohawk haircut. The funny looks and the television was our educator and mentor. Often the term, a dead Indian is the only good Indian, was digested with our morning oatmeal.

Military experience and following construction work all over the U.S. began to open my eyes of understanding about the Native American Indian. All the negative and preconceived ideas of this noble people went out the backdoor with the dish water! I was introduced to a gentle and noble people made up of many tribes (nations). Not only were they horsemen but also farmers, trappers, carvers and fishermen. The Cherokee nation had its own alphabet and printed a newspaper in its language!

A research of this native people revealed the causes of their mistreatment of white people to this day. When politics and broken treaties failed to subdue the Indian nations, then brute force was exercised. Murder the tribal leaders and activists. Abduct the children and re-educate them into the civilized white mans culture. Displace and relocate thousands of people to a distant land. Seize their property, homes, livestock, money and heirlooms.

The anguish, heartache and betrayal of such a noble people cannot be truly conveyed in a story book. To serve the forked tongue and bury the hatchet of disrespect and hatred begins with one person. An honest attempt is made in the following pages to bridge the gap of distrust and set a cornerstone of mutual respect and honor for our Native American Indian.

CHAPTER 1

PACKING FOR TEXAS

The day was looking promising but the lone rider was not ready to start whistlin' Dixie yet. He had been on the trail for only a week now and he was already tuckered out. Job Irvin had left Atlanta, Georgia a week after Christmas on his Grandpa's advice. Pop said it would be cooler, that was a fact, less travelers, and the gnats and skeeters wouldn't be so bad.

Job cleaned his Walker Colt .44, 6 shot pistol and rigged it to the saddle horn plus 50 rounds of ammo. His favorite companion was the handmade skinning knife Pop had fashioned for him a year ago. He had whittled a handle from a deer antler and braded it to a 14 inch blade. Pop had taken time to temper the blade at his homemade bellows and there wasn't a sharper or more durable blade around. A store keep had offered him $20 gold but it was his pride and joy. A lot of time and care had fashioned this pig sticker and he meant to keep it.

Everything else Job owned was stuffed in a canvas poke; an extra shirt and britches, along with his mama's Bible which he kept in an oil cloth. He didn't even own a horse. Pop had give Job one of the 2 mules off the farm along with an old Calvary saddle his great Grandpa had worn out riding with the Continental Army. It was a sight to see but everything he hung on the mule was tried and true, including the mule.

Job wasn't absolutely convinced of his arrangement with the mule yet. Pop was sold out on the dependability of a mule. He assured Job that a mule could be trusted. He said a mule wouldn't do anything to endanger himself and therefore the rider would be kept safe. Pop said they were surefooted, wouldn't make the same mistake twice on the trail, and would find the best places to cross creeks and rivers. That was sure plenty enough pedigree for Job so he took the bridle and Red was his.

Job's family had been through hell and high water the past year in Georgia. Smallpox and measles had taken the lives of his family. He and Pop had been the sole survivors. Together, they had dug a half dozen graves the past year and both agreed there were too many painful memories to stay on the farm. Pop had decided to sell the farm and move to Savannah on the Atlantic Ocean so he could breathe better. Pop was too old for the trail now, besides, you couldn't bribe him to leave his beloved Georgia. He had given Job a mule, a hundred dollars in silver along with his blessing.

Job had heard of a place called Texas out west and decided to seek his fortune there. In 1850 the news from out west was promising. Why, there was free land and a man of color that would work could own his own place.

Pop had been right about the gnats and skeeters not being so bad in the cold weather. The skeeters were still aggravating. Just as soon as the frost had melted along the bay galls and creeks, they started biting. Job used an old Indian remedy that helped. He brought along a skin of lard and smeared it on the back of his neck and hands. He didn't smell too invitin' but it worked on keepin' the bugs away. Other than a bad case of saddle chap, he was managin' well enough.

Pop had mapped out a strategy for Job's trek west. As usual, the old man's advice was right on target and from the looks of things he was gonna need all the help he could get on the trip. This was the slow time of the year for traveling and still it looked like dozens of people on the main roads heading west. There were tater wagons loaded with stoves and what nots, Conestoga's being drawn by oxen and mules, hobos and vagabonds walking, and one wagon loaded with what looked like whores headin' for Birmingham or New Orleans. Job had no choice but to mingle along with the crowd until occasionally the trail opened out into a valley or hollow, then he could leave the road and meander along in sight of the main road.

Pop had warned Job to stay off the main trails and roads heading west. The bushwhacking stories were never ending back east of the peril on the wagon trails. Every town of any size had a sheriff or magistrate to protect the locals. Some towns were far and in between with only an occasional dry goods store at a crossroads. These small communities had their own kind of law, usually vigilante style. A man could get shot, tarred and feathered, or hung for a minor trespass. You didn't touch nobody's chickens, eggs, livestock, or eyeball no white gal. Every wide spot in the road had a jayhawker, bootlegger, or a peddler camped out selling their wares. Vigilante justice was sort of necessary or the lesser of the two evils in the wilderness. The injustice was that they looked at the color of your skin and then figured in the crime. A Chinaman, Indian, or black man travelin' alone didn't stand a chance in hell of a fair trial. Black folks sure enough didn't travel east of the Mississippi. Slavery was the issue nowadays and come to think of it, Job had never laid eyes on a free black person in his life. Anyway, there was no such thing as a fair handshake for a man of color in the Deep South these days.

Job had a secret. That's why he kept to his self and out of town except to post a letter or re-supply his grub. Even though he wore white men's clothes and cropped his hair, his looks were a dead giveaway. Job was part Indian, a breed, and he couldn't disguise the fact. The coal black hair, high cheek bones, and black piercing eyes were a tell tale sign, I'm Injun! Job's daddy, Pop and his daddy had all married Cherokee Indian women. Somehow, the Cherokee blood had all showed up in Job. The only thing Indian Job had on his person was an amulet on a leather string around his neck. There was a fish bone, a single bear claw, and an eagle claw attached to the string. They represented earth, fire, and water and could not be sold or traded. The sacred necklace was over a hundred years old and was to be handed down from one generation to another. It signified the great respect his Mother's clan had for the Great Spirit and for lending them the use of His resources for their livelihood.

The persecution was bad at times for Job's family in Georgia. A lot of folks held it against Job's Daddy for marrying an Indian. Job wasn't allowed in the white school and walked an extra mile to the Cherokee Indian School. They couldn't even practice religion with the white's because many of them believed that Indians and Negroes had no soul. Job knew he had a soul because he often talked with the Great Spirit, especially in the deep woods. He thought he caught a glimpse of the Great One often and would get all warm inside and goose bumps would cover his arms. He never seemed to understand the logic of so called civilized folk when they had so much evidence of the Great One's will in the great book of life, the Bible!

Job's Mother, Nancy, had been his salvation. She was raised in the Cherokee traditions. Her people had developed an alphabet, could read, and even printed a newspaper among the clans. She could write and speak the Cherokee and English language. Nancy had carefully tutored Job in the Cherokee traditions and also knew for Job to survive in a white man's world, he must learn the white man's ways. Job's Daddy, Tad, was a good man and had loved Nancy with all his being. He watched patiently and often with amusement as Nancy would instruct their children about two cultures. Her patience and devotion to the family made his life a lot easier. He could not help what others felt about his choices for a family and there would be no feeling of guilt or shame in his family. Tad taught his family to respect all men and he commanded mutual respect. These choices had left the Irvin family with few friends but those few were loyal.

In the mid 1800's, as some would say, the 7 Cherokee clans in Georgia had seen the hand writing on the wall and ceased their hostilities to keep the white settlers from their tribal lands. They were a cultured and disciplined people that worked together. They settled down as farmers and observed the white man's ways and laws. They learned the legal process, became prosperous, and displayed several wealthy estates. Their passive coexistence lent opportunity to crooked politicians and businessmen that coveted their lands and farms. The white's used violence, betrayal, and political means to dominate and displace the Indian tribes of Tennessee, the Carolina's, Alabama, Georgia, and parts of Florida. The Cherokee clans had suffered the most because of their peaceful and passive ways. Their civil ways was their undoing. In 1830, crooked politicians used the political process to get the Indian Removal Act through Congress. In 1838, 10,000 Federal Troops swept through Georgia and forcefully removed 19,000 Cherokee from their homes and farms. Their homes, farms, and large estates were confiscated by local politicians and merchants. Several hundred managed to escape to the hills of the Carolinas or the swamps of Florida with only the shirts on their backs. The clans were marched a thousand miles west into Eastern Oklahoma and resettled. Over 4000 women, children, and elderly died on what became known as The Trail of Tears!

Job's great grandmother and family had survived only because she was married to a white man. The other reason was great grand daddy Irvin had met the vigilante posse at the creek crossing, armed to the teeth wearing his daddy's Continental cap and jacket. He wore the same colors his daddy displayed when fighting the British and now to keep the vigilantes from stealing his farm and family. The story was that the colors he wore saved the day but most figured it was the persuaders in his belt and long tom across his chest that turned the tide. Great granny said the last words to her before he rode off that day were "Maybe after hell freezes over, but not today!"

Great Granny had expected the worse that day but they survived the roundup. The stories they heard the following week were of countless rapes, beatings, and murder. Not all the whites agreed with or participated in the rape of the Cherokee culture and clans. But not enough stood up and spoke against the Displacement Act. When you have clergy preaching from a pulpit that Indians have no souls and a Congress enacting such a criminal edict with a President signing it into law, what more could be expected?

Something Pop often quoted from the Bible came to mind as Job reminisced. "When the righteous are in authority; the people rejoice; but when the wicked beareth rule, the people mourn. If a ruler hearkens to lies, all his servants are wicked." Proverbs 29:2, 12

Amen to that thought Job. He didn't figure Hell would ever freeze over, so he might as well stand for what is right!

CHAPTER 2

FOOD POISONING

Travelin' had gone pretty good for the first few days. Job was in high spirits and the weather wasn't too bad except for the heavy frost till late morning. He had an 8x8 tarp he could tie up at night as a lean-to to stay dry. There was plenty of kindling and rich lighter pine for a fire. Well before dark, he would begin looking for a place close to water to camp. He'd rinse off as best he could using a little lye soap occasionally. Job would tie his mule close by and if anything or anybody approached the camp, ole' Red would snort, work them ears, and Job would know that they had company. Occasionally there would be a passerby and they would exchange information on the latest news, the trail ahead, or where the next wagon stop was located.

Job had packed along a little smoked venison, hard tack biscuits, coffee, a tin can, and a pound of peanuts. Those provisions didn't last a week and he had spent a whole dollar on grub and corn for the mule. He didn't take to smokin' but he liked a good chew of tobacco often and so did ole Red. He had spent 10 cents on a homemade plug that was really good. The store keep had laid the tobacco leaves out flat in a wooden box. He would paint one side with molasses, add another leaf, and continue the process till there was a stack 3 or 4 inches thick. A thirty or forty pound hickory block was laid on the pile and it pressed eventually down into a solid slab. The "backer" gin was kept in a dark, cool corner, and covered with a tablecloth. A nice plug was cut and wrapped in wax paper. His grub list included rock candy, a pound of soda crackers, a roll of tobacco leaves, one bowl of mulligan stew, and for the mule, a pound of dry corn. All this for one shiny silver dollar!

Highway robbery was Job's opinion of the prices for dry goods. He wasn't a 100 miles out and had already spent a day's wages. He was gonna have to tighten his belt, eat more squirrel and rabbit or work his way to Texas! That would be a good idea if he could find a paying job on the way. Job's plan was to travel to Birmingham, Alabama, drop down to Natchez, Mississippi and cross the river ferry into Louisiana. Word on the trail had it that trouble was brewing in Vicksburg, Mississippi over the slavery issue and he didn't need that kind of trouble.

Pop had a sayin' that "Man's best laid plans are folly." Job was fixin' to have a change of plans. He wasn't two hours out from the last stop at the store when things began to go south. It started with a sharp pain in his bowels. He began to feel sick at his stomach and weak. He raised up a little in the saddle to pass some gas and in one fart he filled his britches with crap. Before he could dismount, he was soiled down to his boots. He staggered to a sweet gum tree he could lean on and kicked off his boots. He dropped his britches while desperately looking for some water close by. Fifty yards away there was a little spring seeping from the hillside. He forked his britches with a branch, grabbed his boots, and hobbled to the spring. It took an hour to clean his self and his clothes while the skiers and weakness got worse. He had the weak trembles before from not eating but never nothing like this. He kicked around best he could to make camp and build a fire but wasn't able to put up the lean to. He hobbled the mule best he could, laid down by the fire, and pulled the tarp over him. All he had on was his shirt and a grim look.

Along about sunset, Job was able to half rig the lean to, rinse the crap off again, nibble on a cracker, and settle in for the night. He thought he would have to die to get better. All through the night he fought the sickness. He would soil himself, stagger to the spring and rinse off, throwing up the crackers and few sips of water he drank, and start the process all over again. He even prayed for God to help him or let him die. He needed relief and the sooner the better. Along about daybreak, he fell into a fitful sleep and had the craziest dreams. At times he didn't know if he was alive or dead. Finally the runs eased off, the dry heaves stopped, and he just laid there peering through the treetops at the cold, blue sky. There was a lot of noise along the branch. Once he thought he heard a dog bark in the distance. Maybe he was still dreaming, he thought as he felt around his pallet to see if he was all there. The stench hit him and he knew he was still in the land of the living! He let out an audible "Thank God" and then just laid there breathing in the cold clean air. The fire had died down long ago and it was cold as a well digger's ass, but he wasn't stirring until the sun was well up.

At noon Job was awakened from slumber by the snorting of the mule. He sensed a presence and felt like he was being watched. He pulled his pistol closer and rolled to his side watching the thicket for any sign of company. His eye caught some color in the blue brush thicket across the branch. A white man with a scatter gun stood watching him from the thicket shadows.

Job raised his hand in a wave as a friendly gesture and managed a weak "Howdy". The man eased out of the bushes and leaped over the stream into the camp. Job continued, "I'm Job Irvin, jest passin' through and come down awful sick. I don't know exactly how long I been out but I figure just one night."

The man, about 30 years old, tall and lean replied, "Tom Hall, this is my place", waving his free hand up and down the creek.

Job laid the pistol on the pallet beside him and said, "I don't mean to trespass and as soon as I can walk I'll be outta here," he defended.

Tom looked around at the poor camp and the half naked man on the ground and said, "You got any open sores or scabs with that sickness?" he asked.

"Nope, jest the runs, chills, fever, and pukin'" Job said.

"Sounds like food pizen, don't eat nuthin' in no sto' in these parts 'cept you see it fixed" Tom replied. "Git yore pants on and pack up, I can help you with yore sickness" Tom instructed kindly. "I'll be back shortly." He turned, jumped the spring, and was gone.

All Job knew to do was comply as he managed to pull his self up beside a tree till he got his balance. He eased around the camp, slipped on the wet pants and boots, rolled everything into the tarp, and tied it the best he could to the saddle. Breaking camp and saddling the mule left Job exhausted so he slid down beside the tree and waited. He didn't know what was in store with this stranger but he wasn't in no shape to resist or argue. He had never been this helpless or at the mercy of a stranger. All he could muster was "God have mercy on me".

Job had dozed off and was jolted awake when Tom jumped back across the spring into his camp. "Can you walk?" he asked. "My place is a mile and a quarter up the creek" Tom pointed to the north.

"Yeah, I think so" Job replied, and belted the pistol while reining the mule behind him. Tom helped Job a little in crossing the spring but kept his distance because of the smell.

Thirty minutes later they stepped out into a cornfield and Job saw a small clapboard cabin at the head of a spring branch. It looked like a shotgun house, meaning you eat and sleep in one big room. There was a mud chimney, lean to front porch with a slab table and wood blocks for seating underneath. Job could make out two kettles out back beneath a red oak tree and a good fire going beneath one. These were homesteaders and they had carved out a pretty nice place thought Job. A young woman and two kids were watching him across the cornfield from the porch. They passed through the cornfield and Tom took the mule lead from Job and hitched it to a sassafras sapling tree.

"This here's Job Irvin", Tom began as he introduced him to his family. "He fell sick on the big road and needs to rest up here a while" he explained. "Job, this is my wife Holly and our chillin', Lucas and Aimee". He gestured to the slim woman and two cotton headed children.

They all nodded and said "Howdy" in unison.

"Foller me" Tom said, and Job fell in behind him as he moved to the back of the cabin. Sure enough, there was the biggest kettle Job had ever laid eyes on in his life, half filled with wash water and a smaller kettle with a good fire under it close by. "Git in the big tub and soak a while and throw yore clothes next to the hot pot over there" Tom instructed.

Job did just as he was told and stepped over into the big kettle. He eased down into the lukewarm wash water and gasped out loud as his chapped butt and legs slipped beneath the lye soaped water. Tom fetched a bucket of hot water from the small tub and poured it slowly into Job's tub. He thought he would just faint from relief as the warm water soothed his aching muscles.

"Thank God" slipped out in a loud whisper as Tom, wearing a silly grin, poured another bucket into the kettle. "For something that feels so good, I wonder why a man will go so long without taking a bath" Tom remarked.

"Too lazy to build a fire," was all Job could say.

"You can wear these clothes of mine till we boil yorn," Tom indicated, pointing to a pile of clothes on a stump. "When you git through come on around to the front an we'll eat fore dark. Holly's fixin' up a mighty fine supper. We don't git no company much out here so she's stretching things".

"Much obliged," was all Job could utter.

Forty five minutes later Job was clean and dressed and kinda baby stepping along the cabin wall making his way to the front porch. He had to lean on the wall for support cause he was so weak from the runs and the effort to clean up. His black hair was sticking out in every direction and the kids were getting a laugh at his expense. Holly admonished them to be polite when he rounded the corner to sit down.

"Make your self at home" Tom said smiling as he pointed out a block for him to sit on. Job obliged.

Everybody found a place at the table and Tom said, "Let's give Thanks." Everyone bowed their heads and listened as Tom began, "Heavenly Father, you let this food grow 'neath our feet, you sent a stranger his company to keep, now with thanks we set down to eat. Amen"

"Jest help your self, Mr. Irvin," Holly offered as she passed Job a heaping plate of fried cornbread. Job was faint from the aroma of the fried food around the table. There was fried squirrel; some kinda field pea, cornbread, molasses, fresh cow milk, and what looked like a winter huckleberry cobbler. This woman had worked a miracle in the wilderness!

"Job, you need to eat all the fried stuff you can hold. It's gonna hurt but there's somethin' bout fried food that helps me overcome sickness an git my strength back quicker." Job just shook his head in agreement as he dug into the vittles.

It was kind of a spectacle watching Job eat, his wild hair stickin' up and his habit of eating meat with his hands.

Tom continued the conversation, "I kilt them squirrel this morning fore I found you" he informed Job.

"Its shore good" Job remarked as he nodded his approval at Holly. He carried on about how good everything tasted and Holly was all red from blushing, but she loved every comment. A kind word in these parts was far and in between. They just never got to see anybody cause they lived off the big road. The kids couldn't believe how much Job liked cornbread. He liked his cornbread with molasses poured over it and he ate it with his meal.

Finally Job couldn't eat another bite but he could feel the strength returning to his spent body. There were all sorts of moans and noises coming from his guts and they were too evident for everyone not to notice.

Tom noticed Job's uneasiness and remarked, "Job, Holly fixed you a pallet on them feed sacks, so you jest lay down there long as you like an we gonna finish up our chores fore dark." Tom pointed at a corner of the porch where there was a neat pile of corn sacks and a homemade quilt laid out.

Job eased to the corner post and knelt down into the sacks. "I don't know what to say to you folks but thanks" he remarked as he nestled into the pallet.

"You don't never mind but rest and git well" Holly said smiling.

Job never remembered anything else as he closed his eyes and fell into the deepest sleep he'd ever known.

CHAPTER 3

PASS IT ON!

Job woke suddenly and was lost as to where he was. It was a warm afternoon and he found him self on someone's front porch. There was a tarp suspended over him. His clothes, knife, boots, and pistol were laid neatly at the foot of the pallet. The pistol had been unloaded and the cartridges laid in a pile beside it. There was a commotion in the cabin. An aroma of something frying drifted out of the doorway. He rolled to his side and saw the two kids, Lucas and Aimee shucking dried corn. Fifty yards out Tom Hall was putting up a split rail fence. Tom saw him stir, dropped what he was doing and strolled that way.

"I see the dead has risen" he quipped smiling, wiping his brow on his shirt sleeve.

"How long was I out?" Job asked as he struggled to get a hold of the corner post and pull him self to his feet.

"You laid down yesterday afternoon. Its past 3 o'clock today" Tom replied. "I don't believe I ever seen a man so tuckered out".

"Well, I shore think you folks saved my life an I hope to never git that sickness agin" Job emphasized.

"Awh, it looked to me like food poison. Don't eat nothin' on that trail west 'cept you see 'em crack the egg." Tom remarked laughingly.

"Don't worry, I lernt my lesson. I'm much obliged the way you folks carried on over me like you did. I'd like to do something to recompense you." Job offered.

Tom cut him off, lifting his hands in refusal said, "We jest done the decent thing an don't mention it agin. I'd knock a dog in the head fore I'd leave him in the shape I found you." he grinned.

"Well I preciate it." Job said looking around. "I got to find me a toilet." he said as he pulled on his boots.

"The outhouse is back yonder an when you git through jest take it easy cause we be eatin' supper fore dark. Your good manner has got Holly fixin all kinda good things for supper." Tom remarked as he went back to work.

Toilet! Job hoped it was close as he walked to the back of the cabin. There past the kettles was a boxin shed made of clap boards with a shake roof top and a plank door hanging by leather hinges. Job made his way past the kettles and opened the door. It was the typical outdoor toilet used by pioneering civilized folks. A hole was dug and the outhouse was built around the hole. A sturdy post was set in the ground in front of the hole that had a short rope with a knot in the end that tied to the post. A feller just dropped his britches, grabbed a hold of the rope, eased back to the edge of the pit, and squatted down to do his business. The knotted rope kept you from falling backwards into the mire. Back in Georgia, Pop had actually built a bench over their pit. He cut a two seater in the top for convenience. One side was for the girls and one for the boys. The boys peed all over their seat and Job had actually tried out the girls nice clean side just to see how it felt!

As Job did his business he reminisced of Pop and the farm. It still hurt too much to think of his parents, brother, and sister. They were always into something in between chores. He and his little brother, Joseph, would lie in wait behind the toilet, and when their little sister Lily or Pop would come out to use it, they would tickle their behind with a long weed. They got a lot of laughs and a couple of scoldings for their shenanigans. You never tickle Mama like that cause Daddy said she'd have a conniption fit and die of a heart attack. Naturally people's first thought was of a black widow spider crawlin' on their backside. We did it anyhow. Pop's toilet had been modern compared to this one. He often said people a come callin' jest so they could visit his toilet to sit down for a good crap.

Job was faint. His gut was already tore up over the back door trots leaving his behind chapped and sore. He was trembling just tryin' to keep a hold of the rope and to keep his legs from cramping. It was a weird thought but if having a baby was anything like this, he'd never put a woman through the misery! Finally, relieved that it was over, he cleaned his self with a pile of moss and sticks left in the corner. There was a neat pile of cut up feed sacks in the opposite corner which he figured was the ladies side. He borrowed a few pieces hoping to make his self presentable.

Slowly and painfully, Job made his way back to the cabin, washing his hands at the kettle. The Hall family was seated and waiting on him to return.

"Howdy, folks" Job said sheepishly sidlin' up to the table.

"Set down there and welcome back to the land of the livin." Tom invited. Everyone else smiled and Job eased down on his block seat hopin' the evidence of what he jest went through didn't follow him to the table. They said thanks over the food and supper started. Job took in the spread and saw that Holly had outdone herself again. There was fried rabbit, cornpone, flour biscuits, field peas, buttermilk, and a dark wild honey in a jar. Everyone got served and Job could tell the children were watching to see what he would do with the fried rabbit. He wasn't going to disappoint them so he spooned a little honey onto his plate, took a rabbit leg, and drug it through the puddle. They watched big eyed as he finished off the rabbit leg and honey. Their parents enjoyed the show too.

Tom said, "Ya'll go ahead and sop some honey but ya gonna eat all of it if you fix it." That's all the two knuckleheads needed to hear so they could try their luck at soppin'.

Tom Hall could tell that Job had some raising. He was curious of where he had come from and where he was headin'. He pressed for conversation hoping to get some answers. "You raised here 'bouts or just passin' through?" Tom asked, spooning a second helping of cornpone. Job slowed up feedin' his face and thought it best to clear the air for these good folks about who they had invited to their table.

"Georgia, born an raised" Job began his story. "Grew up on a farm jest outside Atlanta. Smallpox 'an measles took all my folks 'cept my Grandpa. We had no heart for the farm after we lost everybody. Pop decided to sell out and move to Savannah, Georgia on the ocean. Claimed he could breathe better next to the salt water. I decided to head west to see Texas. I heerd tell they got free land out there."

Tom remarked, "Yeah, that's the story I been gettin'. The Texas government will grant you some land if you become a law abidin' citizen. I also heard it's a wild country out there, lot of lawlessness an such. Well, free land is worth fightin' for. If I was single, I'd probably tag along with you!" Tom stated, casting an assuring smile at Holly.

"Yeah, I think we need you around here a while longer." she emphasized.

Everyone finished supper, the children went off on a wild goose chase, Holly started putting things away for the night, and Tom walked with Job to the spring head to fetch extra drinking water for the house.

"Tom, I can't thank you enough for helpin' git me back on my feet" Job remarked, trying to express his gratitude for the Hall family's kindness.

"Don't never mind Job. That's the good part 'o livin', helpin' your neighbors through hard times. My motto is, Pass it on!" Tom responded as he filled the cypress bucket with the cold spring water. He had staked a cypress box in the pool of cold water and into this he had set a half gallon jug of buttermilk from the supper table. Job noticed a bowl of homemade butter chilling inside the box.

"You saved my life an I feel obliged to you." Job continued. "I'd like to help out some while I am here."

"Don't jump the gun, you still look white around the gills." Tom grinned as they headed back to the cabin. "You're welcomed to do what your able, but don't relapse on me."

"I 'preciate it," Job chimed in, feeling useful again.

For the next week Job eased around the Hall farm and helped out as much as he could. He could feel his strength returning daily. He could almost keep up the pace with Tom. He chinked and daubed the mud chimney with moss and mud, an annual chore now finished. Tom had been working on a split rail fence around the back forty acres. It had been tedious and slow going, for he had to split a dozen rails then put them up. Tom was good with a broad axe. He had Job pounding the wedges when they ran into knots. The mulberry was easy going to split but the ash was kinda ornery at times. They made several trips to the woods for timber. Red, Job's mule, had really been put to the test. Four days, daylight to dark, Job and Tom working together had brought the fence up beside the cabin. The fifth morning, they hung a pole gate to finish the corral. Job declared that even his toenails were sore from swinging the mall. Tom said at least they didn't have to rock Job to sleep at night.

Job had really takin' a likin' to the Hall family but he knew to make it to Texas by Spring, he would have to leave soon. He was two weeks behind schedule, he figured. As much as he dreaded it, he decided to let the family know of his intention to move on.

The next evening at supper, Job breached the subject of Texas to let Tom know that he had decided to hit the trail soon. Tom and Holly were both pioneer folk. They knew that when the bug bit, there was no stopping a feller. The Hall family had a Bible reading and sang a couple songs every Sunday morning after breakfast. That's when Job decided it was best to leave. Everyone would be in high spirits and it would make saying goodbye a lot easier.

Job let Tom know ahead of time. He had his things together and Red, the mule, packed up before breakfast on Sunday morning. He thoroughly enjoyed practicin' religion that morning and even hugged everybody's neck. He had broke into his stash the night before and handed Tom three silver dollars with the instructions to spend two bits on the kids. Tom resisted but after a playful scuffle, he gave in with a lump in his throat. The kids were already hollering about a trip to the mercantile as Job led Red out front of the cabin.

"You got a place to rest anytime and family here if ye ever need us!" Tom remarked as he shook Job's calloused hand.

"I believe that and I'm forever in yore debt" he humbly stated, glancing from Tom to Holly. "I'll post a letter when I git to Texas" he shouted as he mounted the mule, fighting back the tears welling up and the lump in his throat. Holly was crying openly. Tom mustered enough sense to wave Job off. Job couldn't look back as he crossed the corn field heading to the big road and TEXAS!

CHAPTER 4

A HOBO'S ADVICE

Job felt good. He had his strength back, had made some life long friends, and was on his way to Texas. The day was cold and overcast but at least it wasn't raining. He learned from Tom that he was about a two hour ride from the Coosa River and about two days out of Birmingham. He wanted to make the river crossing before dark, maybe get some information about the trail ahead. Job was well fixed for supper because Holly had wrapped up some fried cornpone and tea cakes made with honey. He'd only need a pot of boiling water to make his camp coffee. Some folks called it sock coffee but Job didn't have a spare sock. Travelers would fill a sock with coffee or tea, hang it in a pot of boiling water, till they got the brew desired. The coffee grounds were kept and added to several times, this saved on coffee expense. Job would boil his water then pour the coffee grounds directly into the water. He'd then set the pot aside until the grounds settled to the bottom and pour the coffee. What coffee grounds that didn't settle made for some good teeth pickin' around the campfire later.

Job heard the river crossing before he saw the bridge. Other folks had the same thing in mind, to camp beside the river tonight. There were several freight wagons loaded with lumber, a couple of hobos and no accounts, and two Conestoga wagons loaded with furniture and kids making camp. Job steered clear of the vagabonds and dismounted fifty yards up river from the wagons. He gave a friendly wave at the wagon masters and picked out a spot for the camp. Staking the mule securely,

Job grabbed his canteen and water pot and strolled to the sand bar of the river. Having filled the pot and canteen with water, he eased back to the camp keeping a hand on the pistol, just to let the loafers know he wouldn't tolerate no foolishness.

He broke out the tarp and string and made his pallet. He may not need the lean to for cover but this time of year the weather could change in the blink of an eye. He'd seen a blue northern drop the temperature 30 degrees in an hour. Having a fire started and the coffee pot fixed, Job untied Red and led him down to the river for a drink. It was too crowded here to rinse off, so Job washed his face and hands then strolled back to camp.

Everything was fine and dandy when Job saw a hobo making his rounds to the camper's, asking for leftovers from their suppers. The freight teamsters waved him off but the folks in the Conestoga's handed him a little something to eat. Before long the old hobo was approaching his fire with a toothless grin on his face. He clutched what was left of an old hat in his hands and carried a poke with a strap over his shoulder. Job didn't notice a weapon of any kind but made sure his pistol was handy.

"Evenin' neighbor" the old man offered as he halted just outside Job's space.

"Evenin'" was all Job replied.

"If'n ye got anything left over from yore supper, I'd be obliged" the hobo stated.

The old man had a kind and honest air about him and Job was hungry for conversation. Besides, this feller may know what lies ahead on the trail to Birmingham.

"Got a piece 'o fried pone and what's left of the coffee in that pot, ain't got no extree cup" Job pointed at the fire, inviting the hobo to the leftovers.

The old man's eyes lit up and he shuffled towards the fire as he brought out an old tin cup from his sack. Keeping an eye on Job, he poured ever last drop of coffee and Job passed him the pone.

"Set a spell if ye want" Job offered, pointing opposite the fire.

The old man eased himself down opposite the fire from Job. You'd a thought he held a newborn baby the way he carried on about the vittles. "Much obliged mister" the hobo responded.

They said nothing for a while, mainly because the old man's mouth was full of pone and coffee. Job had not been around the needy very much, being raised on a working farm. Watching the hobo eat was humbling. Something Tom Hall had said after a Bible reading came to mind.

"We don't expect anything in return for helping the unfortunate. I'd jest ask the man to pass the kindness on, that's all, pass it on! Practice charity out of an honest heart and it will always come back to you in some form or fashion." Job had decided right then and there his motto for life would be, "What goes 'round, comes 'round, Pass it on!"

Finally the hobo finished his supper and jest sat there gazing into the fire, like he was remembering a better day. After a good belch he looked at Job and asked, "Headin' west young feller?"

"Yep." Job replied.

"I jest come from outta Birmingham and the sayings still true" the old man said grinning.

"What's that" asked Job, relaxing a bit.

"Be damned ifn' I'd live in Birmingham!" The old man replied with a chuckle.

"Never been there, what's wrong with it?" Job asked.

"Auh nuthin', jest crowded an fast livin'" he replied.

"What's yer name?" Job asked.

"Pete" is all the hobo offered. "Raised south of Tuscyeeloosee on the Black Warrior River. I'm pushing for Atlantee, Georgee and maybe the Big Pond (Atlantic)."

"What's happenin' out west, been to Texas?" Job inquired.

"Nope, I worked as far as the Mississippi River but too much fightin' an such goin' on any further west. It's calmed down a bit since Houston and his bunch whupped Santee Annee and them Mexkins. Texas is part of the Union now they tell me." Pete offered what news he had.

"Well I got a hankerin' to see Texas an maybe settle down out there an raise some cattle an a family" Job offered.

"From what I hear it's a land of opportunity. They tell me a man 'o color stands a dog's chance in Texas. They declare that Mexkins, Aferkins, and Injuns fought along side of the whites in the scrape with the Mexkin army. I never heered the like, whites and coloreds standin' back to back. I'd have to see it to believe it." the old man finished matter of factly.

"Well I aim to see it for myself" responded Job, as he stood and stepped to the edge of the firelight to drain his lizard. "I plan on being there come spring."

"You better build a fire under the ass of that mule 'o yorn cause it's problee five hunnerd miles to the Sabine River. A good horse would take ye five or six weeks!" Pete advised knowingly.

"Five hundred miles?" Job queried, whislin' out loud.

"Yeah, it's 'bout three hunnerd across Mississippi and two or three 'cross Louzana. Plus ye got to know where ya goin'." Pete said.

"Well I aim to push on to Jackson an then drop down to Natchez, Mississippi an cross the big river there." Job answered. Job built up the fire and continued the conversation trying to glean all the information he could from the old hobo.

"I don't rightly know how to say this, an don't take no offense, but ye better keep yore back to the wall an sleep with one eye open west 'o the Mississippi, cause they don't cater to Injuns past there." Pete advised cautiously.

Job unconsciously tensed up and instinctively laid his hand on the pistol as he laid back on the pallet. "How'd you know?" was all Job could muster after Pete had been so blunt and sudden. "Why mister, anybody can look at them eyes an that nose an tell you come from pure stock, Cherokee, I'd say!" Pete retorted.

"Yeah, my Mama and her folks were Cherokee. Grandpa and his Daddy both married Cherokee women." Job explained.

"You a blood alright, an it's best you don't forget it. Course, I don't care what you is. A man's a man till he proves otherwise. I heered a preacher say Hell takes all colors." Pete chuckled.

"What kinda trouble I need to expect on down the trail?" Job inquired.

"Well, the main thing is to stay outta the saloons an cat houses. Don't go waltzin' in the front door 'o no store 'fore ye look. Blacks an Injuns is served at the back door or through a winder most places. Sometimes a sign will point where to go. Why, they won't let a white drifter in the front door of some of them places. An 'fore shore don't go eyeballin' no white gal If'n ya meet on the boardwalk, git off an cross the street. All she got to do is complain an they'll beat the Hell outta ye. Ask 'round fore ye ride into town cause ye may need to go 'round that place. They'll be an Injun camp or black quarter close by the big towns. Jest drop in there an ask 'round fore ye ride on in." Pete was thorough and sincere.

"You got me spooked 'bout my future." Job offered grinning.

"Well, ye shore better pay 'tention if'n ye wanna stay alive. Course, they say thangs is better west of the Sabine but I wouldn't dance on it yet." Pete offered a little hope.

"I'll have my next 'o kin wherever I go." said Job pattin' the Colt .44 on the pallet.

"You'll get to use that thang where yore goin." Pete emphasized the point.

Job got up, took another leak and stoked the fire. "You welcomed to bed down here for the night." Job offered Pete as he fixed his pallet for the night. "I'll take ye up on it" Pete was quick to accept as he broke out a skimpy blanket and positioned the poke for a pillow next to the fire.

Things along the river had settled down. Before long, Job and Pete could be heard snoring and scratching. Job had went to sleep with a lot on his mind concerning what Pete had to say about the trail to the west.

CHAPTER 5

BLUE NORTHER!

Job and the hobo, Pete, were awake long before daybreak taking care of man's business and stoking the fire. You don't travel an unknown trail in the dark even if you are riding a mule. They were shaking everything out and Job sent Pete to the river for coffee water and decided to extend his charity a little further. He broke out the last of the teacakes and set a portion for Pete. The coffee tasted better this mornin', Job figured it was cause he had company. All the jawing had made him feel better and more prepared for the trail ahead.

They drank their coffee and ate in silence for a while. Finally the hobo spoke, "Mr. Job, I ain't one to go slobberin' on ye, but you shore made me feel better 'bout my future. If'n there's any more folks like you in Georgee, that's where I will be drivin' a stake." Pete looked at Job kind of sheepishly.

"Ah, they's more good than bad out there. I'm gonna give you my Grandpa's name and where you might find him in Savanee. If you git that far, tell him I'm OK. He's a mighty good feller and he'll fix you a pallet and a cup 'o coffee."

Job had broke out his pencil and paper to print a note to Pop. He folded the note around a two bit piece and handed it to Pete. Pete carefully unfolded the paper and showed surprise at the two bit piece inside.

"I can't take this Mister. This is a half day's wages 'round here!" he struggled over Job's kind offer.

"Jest pass it on!" Job cut him off, to make him feel better. Pete settled down a bit but never let Job catch his eye. The silence was uncomfortable so Job continued the conversation.

"Anything else I need to know 'bout Birmingham?" Job asked.

Pete was carefully tucking the note and coin in his poke then replied "The main thing is to keep movin' through town. Don't go traipsin' off on no side roads. They's bush whack alleys and some of the storekeeps can't be trusted. If'n ye jest have to stop, keep yore back to the wall. An remember, a grinnin' dog can't be trusted." he instructed.

"I'll keep that in mind." Job said as he kicked dirt over the remaining ashes and checked his packing job in the daylight.

There was a lot of activity along the river as the campers had begun to cross the bridge heading west. Job led the mule down to the water for a drink and a bit of corn. Pete walked along beside him. Job kinda wished they was goin' the same direction and he said as much. "Pete, you could change yore mind an come along with me to Texas. I think we'd make real good pardners." he invited the old hobo.

"Ten year 'go I'd take ye up on it, but I'm too old to cut the mustard anymore. 'Preciate the offer though," he said looking back the opposite way.

Job led the mule to the bridge crossing as Pete ambled along with him. "Don't go mistreatin' no Injuns in Georgia" he grinned, reaching out to shake Pete's hand. He returned the adieu with a firm grip.

"I'll keep that in mind" Pete replied, stepping away from the mule. Job was gonna lead Red across the bridge and they moved out over the river crossing ahead of the Conestoga's. Pete stood waving his old hat till finally he disappeared in all the commotion.

Job crossed the river and now was in the saddle again. He was pushing along at a good trot to get ahead of the wagons and what dust was raised. It didn't take long till he was well enough ahead of the crowd and able to relax a bit and reminisce.

The comment that Pete had made about him lookin' Cherokee got Job thinkin' about Tom Hall and his family. Not one word or comment had been made concerning his roots. They bound to have known that he was Indian but never mentioned or acted funny to him. He did recall one day when the children were playing cowboys and Indians. The Indian was always the loser and the one that was shot. During one shootout Lucas, the cowboy, had shot the Indian, Aimee, and had popped off, "Die, you no count savage!"

Tom was at his side immediately, gave an apologetic look at Job, but never said a word. It all added up now. They had known all along but never brought it up. It did not matter to the Hall's! They were as white as you could git but treated him with great kindness and respect as a human being. Job promised himself to never forget that there are good folks in the world. It was his job to pass it on!

Wolf Creek was just another wide spot in the road between the river crossing and B'ham. Riding pass the mercantile store, Job noticed it was a mail stop. He wanted to post a letter to Pop and purchase a few dry goods for the trail. He planned on riding straight through B'ham with no stops or detours. He reined the mule to the front side of the store where he could see the mule from the inside. He dismounted and half hitched Red to a rail.

The usual bunch of idlers was hanging around the front porch, a couple of no accounts bummin' 'baccer from the customers exiting the store and a wine-o propped up beside the building, sound asleep. It was amusing cause the flies were cleaning his teeth in his stupor. A couple old men were playing cards atop a tater box and a half a dozen Negroes were cleaning and oiling harnesses beside the store. One feller was beating out time on a banjo and singing his joyful tune. Job never tired of the Negro spirituals and jivin' tempo music they played. Back in Georgia, he had often visited the Negro quarters on the big plantations and listened to the players on Sunday evenings. They could take a banjo, a metal bucket, washboard, spoons or dry bones, and produce the most amazing sounds. There was always singing and dancing. You couldn't help but notice how similar their culture was to his own Cherokee roots. He had made some good friends among the Africans.

The banjo player noticed Job's appreciation for the music so he really put on a show! None of the whites made eye contact with him but he could tell that he was being scrutinized and weighed in the balance. He moved on inside the dark store room to scout for his needs. He picked up a circular on the local news and told the store keep what he needed to purchase. The store keep shuffled around to the several kegs of dry goods. He weighed out his coffee, crackers, and a pound of corn for the mule. He also ordered three plugs of tobacco after he lifted the cover of the gin and smelled it. He bought a piece of script and an envelope so he could write a note to Pop giving his location and welfare. He posted the letter to Savannah, paid for the dry goods, and then made his way outside.

Things got quiet when Job exited the store. He walked to the mule and stowed away the vittles. Taking a plug of the sweet tobacco, he walked back past the porch to the alley where the Negroes were gathered. The banjo player was tuning the banjo. Job walked over and handed him a chaw that he had sliced off the plug of tobacco. The feller gave Job a hundred dollar smile as he popped the chaw into his mouth and commenced to playing. You could read the desire on the men cleaning the harnesses so Job passed the plug to one of them and eased back toward the mule. He could hear the scrambling among the Negroes for a piece of the tobacco. He felt good about it as he cleaned his knife on his pants leg.

Job could sense the resentment from the bums leaning on the porch as he walked by them. He heard one mumble something about an "Injun" so he laid his hand on the butt of the pistol as he approached the hitching rail. He retrieved a handful of corn and fed it to Red, never taking his eye off the bums.

He heard one say louder, "Now where you thank an Injun got a fine mule like that?" The sarcasm was intended and public.

Job swung up into the saddle, looked at the bums, and in a loud, clear voice said in fluent Cherokee, "Even the wild animal hunt for food to feed their family. You lazy like dog."

He reined Red around and rode away. The bums got all excited and he could hear them cussing. From the corner of his eye, he could tell the Negroes got a kick out of what he said though no one knew what it meant.

Job found out first hand the true meaning of what Pete, the hobo, had said, "Be damned if'n I'd live in Birmingham!" The crowded streets, noise, mud, and stink was overwhelming. It was ever man for himself! The jayhawkers were constantly tugging trying to peddle something. There were two story buildings stacked one against another, allowing no air circulation. Every breath was putrefying! He pressed on for an hour before the crowd thinned out. He had tied a handkerchief over his nose and mouth and was now able to remove it to get a breath of fresh air. Red, the mule, even perked up into a better mood. He held to the main road through town then he saw a clapboard sign with an arrow pointing west to Meridian, Mississippi. He wanted to clear the town so he could find a place to camp by the water tonight. He was dirty and tired but pushed on for another hour. At the base of a little hill, he noticed a small boxin' church recently whitewashed with a small graveyard out back. In a draw below the church was a running creek, so he rode on by and dismounted. While the mule drank, he scouted out a place to camp. He broke out the lean to and built a fire. While the coffee water boiled, he gathered up enough kindlin' wood for the night and rinsed off best he could in the cold creek. He felt better as he settled back on his pallet with a cup of steaming coffee. The crackers didn't make much of a supper but he promised himself a roasted rabbit or squirrel the next day. There was a little change in the weather a comin' cause he had heard a screech owl way off in the distance. An owl screechin' this early in the evening was a sure sign of weather change. Job hoped he was ready as he dozed off to sleep.

Job was jolted awake. The tarp was flapping and a low moan could be heard in the tree tops. The north wind was like ice and sleet was rattling the leaves all around. The fire was long out when Job began packing in the dark. The cold was numbing. Job knew he had to find a windbreak or solid shelter fast. This was a blue Norther' and it could blow all night or three days. He remembered the church, untied Red and moved to the building. Having tied Red on the south side out of the wind, Job made for the front door and shoved it open. He stepped inside, stood in the dark till his eyes adjusted enough to make out a half dozen slab benches and a block pulpit. Shoving three of the benches together, he arranged a pallet out of the tarp and blankets. Racing back outside in the cold, he unpacked the mule and toted the gear back inside the church. He took one more trip to secure Red, take a leak, and made it back to the pallet. He rolled up in the quilts, clothes, boots and all. Things settled down a bit and then he heard some scampering on the floor of the church. He wasn't the only one seeking refuge from the storm. He felt like a chicken on the roost but at least he was above the critters on the floor. Sometime later he warmed up enough to doze off. The last thought he had was that next time he would pay heed to the screech owl's warning!

CHAPTER 6

RESCUE!

At daybreak, through the cracks in the ceiling, Job could see clear blue sky. That meant the blue Norther had blowed through. It would warm up a little later on in the day and that made Job feel better. He unwrapped from the cover, shook everything out, and packed it all together. The day was looking promising as he stepped outside into the sunlight, but something just wasn't right. He stretched real good, looking around at the frozen ground and sleet covered leaves. He stepped to the side of the building to relieve himself and kept this nagging foreboding.

Job moved to the south side of the church and came wide awake! Red was missing! Maybe he just pulled loose in the storm and wandered off. He scouted around with no luck and came back to where Red was tied the night before. There was a boot print on top of the sleet. Someone had been here before daybreak, after the sleet had stopped falling. A horse thief had snatched the mule!! That's all Job needed now, was to lose his ride. He knew time was critical and retrieved his gear from the church. Moving to a blue brush thicket on the creek, he hid everything except his pistol, ammo, canteen, and a handful of crackers. His trusty skinning knife was still tucked inside his boot. Job filled the canteen in the creek, ate a cracker, and washed it down with a cold drink of water.

Moving back to the church, Job picked up on the mule tracks heading up the creek and away from the big road. That was good, cause if the thief made it to B'ham, he would never find his mule. He knew it would be useless to look for a lawman to help out because it would be his word against the thief. All the law would see was that he was a Blood and walk away. One thing Job had on his side was that the mule was marked. Pop marked all his livestock, to keep the thieves honest, he said. Red's left ear had been pierced. You had to know where to look so's to find the hole.

At first, Job was seething mad, but then what his daddy and Pop had taught him surfaced and he calmed down. He was a natural tracker and hunter and began to think cool and sober. His daddy, Tad, had said it was alright to get excited or mad, but don't let it control you. Channel the energy into positive action. Keep cool, breathe deep, and don't react but plan every step. Whether it was game or an enemy you are tracking, get to know them. Take your time, watch, and listen. Let the wildlife and forest around you, be your friend. The wind will bring you clues to the unseen.

Two things you didn't trespass against back in Georgia, a man's family or livestock. A thief would hope to get caught by the sheriff because if the local's caught one, they would either beat him half to death or tar and feather him. The latter was worse than the beating, for it took a lot of kerosene and months to wear it off and heal from the blistering. Job remembered one incident where a horse thief's ear was cut off, just like marking a hog. Job didn't want to hurt anyone but he was gonna do whatever it took to git it done!

The trail the thief was leaving was easy to follow. A quarter mile up the creek he had taken an old wagon road up a shallow hollow. He was brave or else an idiot for there was tobacco spit ever now and then. He had stopped to piss in the road and there was a steam cloud rising from the cold ground. Job knew he was dangerously close and he moved stealthily along the edge of the wagon trail stopping often to listen to the forest. A faint hint of smoke hung in the air. When the cold wind would gust, he would move along to the rustle of the leaves and tree branches. A gray squirrel in the distance was barking and Job knew something had disturbed it. Several more squirrels took up the barking and whistling further away and Job knew he was close to the thief. He couldn't be over a hundred yards away and Job was gritting his teeth in anticipation.

Fifty yards down the trail the hardwood forest opened up into a little clearing. A small cabin stood in the clearing next to a spring branch. Downstream from the cabin was a hog pen and Job could see two shoats rooting inside. There was a woodpile in front of the door and smoke coming from the mud chimney. There was no sign of his mule but he could hear a crow fussing behind the cabin and decided to swing behind and see. Sure enough, he caught a glimpse of Red tied to a rail next to the back door. He didn't want Red to see or smell him because he would try to come to him and give his position away.

Job wanted his mule back in one piece but he also wanted some kind of justice for the thief. If Red scented him, all hell would break loose so he moved back to the front of the cabin. Activity was picking up inside the cabin and smoke was boiling out of the chimney. The thief was probably hungry, bless his soul, thought Job. He would receive a little something extra with his breakfast this morning. He made a run for the wood pile beside the front door and sprawled flat beside it and listened. He could hear a man talking inside the cabin.

Easing up to the only window in the place, Job sneaked a peek inside. It was dark and shadowy and took a minute for his eyes to adjust to make out what was inside. There was a dirt floor, a slab post bed in one corner, a slab table with a couple of blocks for seats next to it. The fireplace had a waist high shelf with a skillet and a Dutch oven on top. An old iron grate was atop the fire and a huge skillet in use.

Job's senses couldn't register to what he saw tending to the fireplace at first. The most pitiful and dirtiest white girl he had ever seen was squatting next to the hearth. She was red headed with fair complexion being probably twenty years old. What made Job's blood run cold was the shackle around her ankle and a chain linked to a plow ring attached to a stake buried in the floor. A ten foot chain gave her access to the fire and pallet nearby. The girl's left ankle was bruised from the shackle and both feet were mangy looking. She had been captive for a while from the looks of things. Something was bad wrong here and every ounce of decency in Job rose up to meet the challenge. The mule was critical to Job's livelihood and trip to Texas but the bondage of this girl overshadowed everything.

Job had heard stories of white slaves in the Great Smoky Mountains and out west but never so close to civilization. What was ironic was this man would be hung on site for enslaving this white girl and the same people would go home to a dozen men, women and children of color shackled in the same manner. He couldn't tolerate none of it, that's one reason he was leaving Dixie.

Making his way back behind the woodpile, Job was laying out a plan that would secure his mule and free the girl. One thing to his favor was there seemed to be no dog around. What would keep a dog alive at this rundown shack, he thought disgustedly. A man may be poor but there was no excuse for being filthy and lazy. The pigs even looked underfed as he surveyed the area.

A myrtle bush had grown up beside the south side of the cabin wall and Job had decided to have another look inside the shack before he made a move to execute his plan. He wanted to make sure the man was alone and see what kind of weapon he carried. He could hear mumbling inside and so he made a dash for the south wall. Crouched beside the half chinked poles, he looked for a crack to peep inside. A peephole wasn't hard to find because the cracks between the logs had never been maintained with mud and moss since its construction years ago. Job scanned the one room cabin for weapons or any other surprises he might have to deal with later. There was a corn shuck mattress and nasty looking wool blankets on the slab post bed. The walls were bare and next to the table were several wooden kegs, probably dry goods. Next to the front door what looked like a Colt Dragoon hung in a holster on a wooden peg. Job couldn't make out another weapon in the room. The man probably had a knife on his person.

Job heard the feller before he saw him. He spoke to the girl in a loud command, "Fry up some pork and bile me some coffee water!"

The young woman never looked up but set about fixin the scoundrels vittles. He stepped out of a dark corner and went to rummaging through the kegs and brought out a sack of coffee. He tossed a slab of salt pork from one keg to the girl. She began to whittle pieces of the pork off the slab with a case knife barely three inches long. The man picked up a dishpan and walked to the front door and tossed the dirty water outside. A cypress barrel beside the door contained the kitchen water and he rinsed the pan and refilled it with clean water. Back inside he placed it next to the fireplace and the girl drew her coffee water from the pan.

The thief looked to be in his forties and was of medium build. A scraggly beard covered his face and dark oily hair hung to his shoulders. He was wearing overalls and heavy boots with a ten inch skinning knife strapped to his left side. Job had his work cutout for him and he realized this was going to be a life or death struggle when it started. He needed the advantage of surprise and decided to wait till the man had eaten and got careless to make his move. He settled back against the wall and took a pull from his canteen and checked his pistol and skinning knife. He was as ready as a man could be and listened to the preparations inside the cabin. The frying pork and coffee brewing made his guts growl.

31

Hearing the pans rattle, Job took another peek and saw the man feeding his face at the table. The pitiful girl was sitting beside the hearth with a piece of fried pork and a tin cup of coffee. Job had seen hunting dogs chained and fed like this but never a human being. Wild animals in the woods lived better than this. At least they come and go as they please, Job thought.

Ten minutes later, the man had finished eating and was laid out across the bed. The girl was gnawing on her pork and sipping the coffee. Things were just the way Job wanted them and he decided to make his move.

Having picked out two good chunks of firewood, Job eased to the corner next to the front door and threw one as far as he could away from the cabin. There was a loud thump as the chunk hit the ground and a quite pause inside the cabin. Job threw the other piece in the same direction and waited. He heard the old bed creak and footsteps as the man reached the front door. Through the peephole Job saw the man pull the Colt from its holster as he opened the front door. He looked around once and then walked out past the woodpile in the direction of the noises he heard.

In three strides Job was behind the thief and barked an order, "Freeze mister and don't turn around!" Job commanded.

"What the hell?" the man said as he froze in place, the pistol out to his side.

"I come for my mule you theivin' bastard!" Job spoke through clenched teeth.

"What you talking 'bout mister, that mule wandered up here, I ain't took nobody's mule." he defended.

"Yeah! He wandered alright, with yore boot tracks leadin' him!" Job replied.

"Look mister, we can fix this, jest git yore mule an leave." the man pleaded.

"Can't do that pardner, I'm taking that white slave you got chained up in there, so lay that widow maker and pig sticker on the ground real easy and git back inside!" Job instructed.

The thief half squatted and laid the pistol and knife on the ground then slowly turned to face Job.

"Well I be pissed! A Injun bushwhacked me on my own place!" he scowled.

"Don't push your luck, just move on inside and git that girl loose!" Job ordered.

32

Cursing under his breath, the thief walked past Job and stepped through the door. Job followed a step behind with the Colt 44 at his lower back. As the man stepped inside he sneaked a jerk on the strap latch and slammed the door into Job's gun causing him to fall against the door jam. The pistol slipped from Job's hand and without time to retrieve it he dove for the thief's backside as he leaped for the table and the case knife the girl had laid down. Job knew this was a life or death struggle and laid into the back of the man's head with his fists. The man stumbled and Job drove his left knee into his lower back while grabbing a choke hold with his left forearm in one leap. They both fell to the dirt floor in a heap and somehow the feller twisted around enough to knee Job in the stomach. This blow knocked Job breathless and he blindly came around with a right fist and caught the man square over his left ear, bursting the ear drum while splitting the earlobe wide open. The feller screamed in pain and before he closed his mouth Job came up with a left fist and slammed into his front teeth. Job felt the teeth cave in and blood splattered into his face.

The man rolled into a fetal position to protect himself from Job's onslaught but it was all over. Job staggered up and off the man wiping slobber and blood from his face and hands. He looked around to get his bearings and saw the girl had pulled away from the fight as far as the chain would let her.

Stepping back to the front door Job picked up his pistol and asked the girl in an urgent tone, "What's going on here Mam? I need to know so I can help you!" he pressed for an answer.

After several attempts to speak through quivering lips she managed to respond, "I'm Angie, an this feller snatched me from my family a couple a months ago." She began to tremble and cry softly as everything overwhelmed her.

The thief on the floor began to vomit and spit the broken teeth up and Job saw blood seeping from the ear canal.

"Where's the key to that shackle, Mister?" Job asked, pointing the pistol into his face.

The man fished around his pocket and brought out the key. Job snatched it and stepped beside the girl handing her the key. She was out of the shackle and at the front door in a flash.

"Jest hold on Miss, we are not finished here yet." Job said to her.

"Roll over here!" Job ordered, motioning to the man to move next to the hearth. The feller scooted next to the hearth and lay whimpering.

"Don't move a muscle! Now Mam, you git over here and fix that shackle to the feller's right leg!" He instructed the girl.

She hesitantly shuffled next to the man on the floor and squatting down, she clamped the shackle around his right ankle and it locked shut with a hard click. She immediately rose and moved back to the front entrance.

Job moved to the table and picked up a bag of silver coins and the poke of coffee.

"You can't leave me here like 'dis, I'll starve to death!" the man pleaded.

"Good riddance!" Job retorted, walking to the door and ushering the girl out ahead of him. He handed her the bag of coins and coffee, then retrieved the man's pistol and knife lying on the ground. Moving to the rear of the cabin, Job untied the mule, who was all ears and eyes at the sight of his master. Job gave him a quick scratch on the head and walked him back to the front of the cabin.

Turning to the girl he said, "Angie, I need you to ride my mule so we can make tracks out a here, this nut may have friends!" He made a clasped finger stirrup and helped her to the back of the mule. Red was a little shy but settled down. Job couldn't help but notice how bad this girl smelled but tried to pretend otherwise.

Job could hear the chained thief thrashing around inside the cabin and walked to the open door. He wanted to leave the feller with something to think about for the next few hours.

"I'm reportin' this matter to the Sheriff and turnin' the girl over to them. It might be better to starve to death, cause you know what they'll do to a white slaver!" Job emphasized the latter.

Job could hear the chained man yell for a quarter mile back down the branch as he led the mule and rider back to the church.

CHAPTER 7

ANGIE

Sometimes doing the right and decent thing can be downright dangerous. Job had a complicated matter on his hands. He needed to finish the job and deliver the girl, Angie, to safety. He wanted to make sure she reached the civil authorities but with him being left unknown. When word got out the focus would be a white girl in the company of an Indian. Too much could go wrong for his sake and he decided to find the first farm and leave the girl there on the trail west.

Arriving back at the church, Job rounded up the gear he had hidden, repacked everything and situated Angie behind him on the mule. He needed to make tracks as far as possible in case the thief broke loose from the shackle and pursued them. Job figured he would have to disable or even kill the man if they met again. Taking no chances he pushed the mule for an hour without the first sight of a farmstead and dark was upon them soon.

One thing good about this part of Alabama was there were plenty of springs and creeks with good water. Job found a wet place in the trail and followed it to a spring bubbling from the side of a hill. There was a nice deep pool at the source and he dismounted, helped Angie down and began to make camp.

Turning to Angie he said, "You sit next to that pool of cold water and soak that bad ankle while I make camp."

She limped to the waters edge and began to bathe her swollen ankle and dirty feet. She was conscience of how dirty she was and was taking a raccoon bath, Job noticed.

Job managed to rig up a pretty good private shelter for the girl. His plan was to help her get clean again without any more embarrassment. This young woman had already suffered a lifetime of abuse in a couple of months and Job felt obligated to help restore her dignity. He built up a good fire, broke out his extra pair of britches and shirt and said to the girl, "Mam, I'm gonna walk off toward the big road and while I'm gone, you take that piece of soap and clean yourself up. You can wear that set of clothes till we get something better. Just take your time and give a yell when you git finished." Job continued as he checked his pistol and started down the branch. "I'll fix some coffee and vittles soon as you git through."

"Yes, Sir!" was all Angie was able to say for Job was out of sight in a moment. She set about cleaning up as fast as possible. She couldn't help but weep as she scrubbed away the stink and filth of her oppressor. The shirt and pants were way too big so she rigged a suspender from a strip off her old dress. She dropped the remainder of the tattered and dirty dress into the fire and felt a sense of relief watching it burn. She decided at that moment to burn that bridge and focus on the help she had at hand. This feller, Job, was a decent and kind person and she was not going to add to his burden by whining and complaining.

Job had found a spot close to the big road and settled down on a fallen log to rest and get his thoughts together. His plan was to keep watch between cat naps through the night in case the thief was in pursuit. He had not planned on being a hero but the chips had fallen this way and all he could do was to make the best of the situation. He was daydreaming about Georgia when he heard Angie give a little shout and he eased back toward the camp.

Other than the smell of smoke you could not see the campfire from the big road and that was good. Angie had added wood to the fire and had water on to boil when Job walked up. He couldn't help but grin at the sight of the skinny girl in his big clothes. He noticed she wouldn't look him in the face and decided to break the ice for her.

"You cleaned up mighty good, there Mam." He stated while digging out the coffee and crackers. He noticed the swelling had gone down on her ankle. Measuring his coffee grounds into the boiling water, he set it aside to brew. He handed the girl a few of the crackers and said, "This is all I got to eat till tomorrow. Hep yourself to the coffee," and he handed her his cup.

She took the cup and poured the coffee. Turning to Job, she offered him the coffee and said, "I'll drink some later, but not till you've had yours."

He took the hot brew and she sat down next to the fire and began to munch on the dry crackers. Job ate a half a dozen crackers and washed them down with the strong coffee. He poured another half cup and passed it over to the girl. She took the cup never looking up at Job.

"Thank ye," she said.

Job watched her eat a while and decided to get some information on her so he could make plans for the next day.

"I'm Angie Cooper, and I'm from Tuscyloosy, not far from here. Me and my folks haul taters an' corn to B'ham to sell. We always stop at the church to rest an sometimes spend the night. We was there bout two months ago. I had walked up to the crick to tend to woman's business. I 'member seein' this feller in the woods an he asked me what I was doin' out there. I tried to tell him an I guess he knocked me in the head, cause I waked up chained to his floor." She paused like it hurt to remember any further.

"I 'member men comin' by lookin fer me but he had me gagged an hid till they left. He never let me loose cept for woman business or to try and force a poke. Said he'd kill me ifn' I even thought about leavin'!" She literally was trembling as she finished.

Job waited a while before pressing for more information. Finally he spoke.

"You bein' form Tuscyloosy makes things a lot simpler. I be goin' that way and if you know anything bout the trail jest tell me." He encouraged her.

It seemed to make her feel better to talk so she started off by saying, "I know this road like the back of my hand. Our farm is no more than two days ride from here." She emphasized, not able to keep the tears back, just thinking of her mama and daddy. Wiping her eyes on the shirt sleeve, she continued, "About two hours from here is Johnson's Mercantile. We always stop there and add a little freight to our wagon if they got any. Daddy makes a dollar extry helpin' that a way. They be good people an they know'd me all my born days." Job could see life coming back into her eyes and was glad of the good news. Maybe things would take a turn his way for a change.

Job had fixed a pallet beneath the tarp for the girl and pointed it out to her.

"You sleep there on that pallet and I'm gonna stand watch between naps till daylight. If we have compnee you stay put and let me handle it." He instructed Angie.

"You think that man is following us?" she asked.

"I doubt it, but he's one crazy bastard. Don't you fret none, Mam, If he shows up here I'm gonna put 'em down!" Job was surprised at his own words, but meant what he said.

"Git you some rest, Mam." Job remarked, and walked out of the camp light into the shadows along the spring. He waited to give the girl space to get comfortable. He eased along the big road taking in the night sounds. Slipping back into camp, he found Angie sound asleep and fixed a place to lean back facing the big road. The toil and stress of rescuing his mule and the girl had worn Job to a frazzle and he was out like a candle in minutes.

The night passed quietly and Job was awakened by a grey squirrel jumping through the tree limbs above the spring. It had just turned light and it was cold as a frog. Job eased off into the bushes to take a leak and then commenced building a good fire. He had promised himself some kind of roasted meat two days ago and he was gonna fulfill that promise today. Angie had awoke and was watching him fix the fire.

"Mornin." He gestured a nod at the girl.

"Good mornin', Mr. Job" she replied.

"I'm gonna shoot a few squirrel or maybe a cotton tail while you get up and about." He said to Angie.

"If you don't mind, make a pot 'a coffee." He asked her as he took his pistol and walked up the holler above the spring.

In less than an hour Job was back in camp with four grey squirrels strung together. He noticed the coffee was made and Angie had shook the tarp and blankets out and rolled everything together. She looked a heap better than yesterday Job thought to himself.

"Mornin," he said, "You feelin' better today?" he asked her.

"Yes sir," she replied, "I must have died on you, last night." She said.

Job tossed the squirrels on the ground at the spring and moved to the fire to warm up. Angie handed him a cup of the steaming coffee.

"Hep me skin these squirrels and we'll have a good breakfast before we head out." Job told Angie.

"I be glad to." Angie said as she walked to the spring to sort out the squirrels for cleaning.

Job finished the coffee and joined her at the spring. Picking up a squirrel, he positioned the two back legs for her to hold. Gripping the squirrel tail he made a half moon cut and telling her to hold on, he pulled the skin all the way to the front feet. He snapped the front ankles, cutting both free with the head. Having her swap ends, he pulled the hide from the rear quarters and tossed it away. She again held the hind legs, careful not to get hair on the fresh meat and Job gutted the critter. Ten minutes later the squirrels were cleaned, washed and Job was staking two of them over the fire. He broke out more crackers, a pouch of salt and added more water to the coffee pot. He realized just how hungry he was as the smell of the roasted meat drifted from the fire.

An hour later Job had broke camp, packed everything on the mule and he and Angie were following the creek back to the trail west. They had made short order of the roasted squirrel and finished off the crackers and coffee. Job would need to re-supply today or have a miserable camp that night. Making the big road, Job fed the mule a little corn and advised Angie to take care of her woman's business if needed. He wanted to make tracks today and especially reach the mercantile before dark. When all was ready Job mounted the mule and pulled Angie up behind him. They made good time for the next hour and decided to give the mule a break so they walked a while. They passed a couple of cabins and met a few travelers but Job didn't want any contact with strangers, besides they could be followed and the thief would be seeking information of their whereabouts.

Sometimes after high noon, Angie perked up and said they were not far from the country store. Sure enough, they topped a little hill and there was the mercantile at the crossroads. Job could sense the excitement as Angie stretched to see what lay ahead.

"That's it, Mr. Job, the Johnson store!" she almost squealed.

Job said a silent prayer that this would go well for his sake as they rode up to the front porch.

CHAPTER 8

JOHNSON'S STORE

The world seemed to stop as Job and Angie rode up to the hitching post in front of the store. A couple boys were playing marbles beside the store and they froze at what they saw. One boy broke loose from his trance and ran screaming for the front door of the store.

"Pa! Ma! She's alive, it's her Pa!" the boy could be heard yelling inside the store.

There was a mighty commotion inside the store and suddenly a middle aged man followed by a hefty looking woman rushed out onto the porch. Both were big eyed and mouths gaped open and the woman cried, "Glory be! Angie Cooper, why we done buried you girl!" she exclaimed.

Ben Johnson, the store keep, was carrying a scattergun and kept his eye on Job as they dismounted the mule. Angie was crying out loud and laughing as she rushed into the outstretched arms of Mrs. Johnson. Everyone just stood their ground and watched the women hugging and crying for like five minutes. Finally, everyone settled on the front porch on stools and blocks. Mrs. Johnson sent the boys for a bucket of drinking water and soon Job and Angie were refreshed by the cool well water. Angie was finally able to stop the tears of joy and get her thoughts together enough to tell her story.

"I was kidnapped! All this time I been chained like a dog in a man's house." She spoke soberly.

"Why, we all thought you was stole away and kilt by a panther or something." Mrs. Johnson said.

"That probably would a been better." Angie tearfully replied.

"We had stopped to rest at a church creek this side of B'ham an this feller knocked me in the head and kidnapped me. Mr. Job came along and rescued me and his mule." Angie gestured at Job, with gratitude written all over her face.

Job couldn't help but blush but was relieved the truth was coming out about his part in their affair.

Mr. Johnson finally spoke, "My Lord girl, we searched these parts for a month and never found a clue to yore whereabouts. It nearly kilt yore Ma and Pa. Yore Ma hadn't got over it yet. She shore needs to see you. I think this is gonna put things right in their lives again."

Turning to Job he continued, "Mister, you done a service to this family. We all are obliged to you." He reached out and shook Job's hand with both of his hands.

Job just looked at the floor and mumbled, "Thank you."

"It's still a half days ride to the Cooper farm so you welcomed to rest here tonight. We'll fix you a good supper and I think the wife can fix Angie up with another set of clothes." He said grinning at Angie's baggy pants and shirt.

"I could shore use a good supper and a bar of soap, if it's alright with Angie." Job replied.

"Yes sir, its fine with me." She consented, and everyone set about making arrangements.

Mrs. Johnson put the boys to work drawing water for the bath tub then led Angie to the back of the store to the living quarters.

Job set about unpacking and feeding the mule. He fetched a bucket of water for the mule and spent a little time checking his hooves and scratching his head. Besides grampa, this mule was the closest kin he had in the world and he meant to take good care of him.

Mr. Johnson joined Job as he groomed his mule and Job related to him the thief and the rescue of Angie Cooper. He described the thief and the location of the cabin.

"Sounds like a feller called Nettle. I've seen him a couple of times. He's a no account that slouches around B'ham, a thief and a bum. I'm gonna send fer the constable in B'ham and take care of that no account. From the trouble he caused in these parts, I don't figure he'll be seeing no judge, jest the undertaker!"

Job could feel the cold sincerity of Mr. Johnson and knew justice would be served. Job doubted the thief would ever be found or seen again in these parts but didn't say anything.

The country store was a beehive of activity all evening and Job tried to stay out of the way and tend to his own rat killing. He browsed around the store and re-supplied his grub and feed for the mule. An old Calvary saddle bag caught his eye and he included it in his purchase. With the saddle bag he added a tin plate and another cup. He didn't want to get too fancy for the trail but he was learning that a few basics sure made life easier in the wilderness. He was gonna have to improve his diet or he might get sick. He threw in a roll of fishing line and a half dozen hooks.

Job had made a neat pile of his purchases on the counter when Mr. Johnson said, "They's a fifty dollar reward for Angie's whereabouts and you'll be collecting it." He informed Job.

Job was completely taken aback and replied, "No sir, I can't do that, I jest did what was right. Just tell em to do what the Good Book says and pass it on!" he said matter of factly.

"Its government money and you need to take it. You risked yore life and besides this ain't over yet. You git everything you need and I'm gonna write it up and will deduct it from the reward." He instructed Job.

"Well, we'll see. I'm nearly a week behind schedule getting to Texas and I can't wait around for the constable. I need to make them river crossins before the spring rains." He explained.

Mr. Johnson had it all figured out. "I'm the postmaster in these parts and I thank I can write up an official paper with my seal on it and you'll be able to git your part of the reward in Tuscyloosy. I'll send them the bill for these dry goods along with you." He explained.

"I wasn't expecting nothing like this, though I could use the help." Job accepted the offer.

After learning of his good fortune, Job went back to shopping and throwed in another pair of pants and shirt and two pair of socks. You talk about living high on the hog. He noticed a fancy pinafore on the women's shelf and laid it besides his purchase. While he was figuring up everything there was a shuffle to the back of the store and he turned to look. He couldn't believe his eyes. There stood the girl he had rescued but she was transformed into the prettiest thing he'd ever seen since leaving Georgia. She was wearing a blue flowered feed sack dress with a little white collar and ruffled sleeves. Mrs. Johnson had combed her red hair back to a bun in the back. That red hair next to the fair complexion and blue dress made Job's heart pound. He was speechless and just stood drinking in her beauty. She just smiled at everyone and shifted around on bare feet. Mr. Johnson broke the uncomfortable but amusing silence.

"My God! Where'd you come from? Is that you Angie?" He exclaimed and walked over to give her a hug.

Mrs. Johnson was just beaming with joy at the way Angie looked and the surprise on the men's faces.

Job was still at a loss and finally said, "You sure are different . . . I mean purty!" He fumbled for words.

Everyone laughed and Mrs. Johnson advised the men to be ready to eat supper in an hour. Mr. Johnson sent the boys to draw more water for Job's bath and led him to the back of the store to the boiling pot. The set of Job's clothes that Angie had been wearing was already washed and hung out to dry. Mr. Johnson showed Job the white oak tub and soap and left him to clean up. He took Job's dirty clothes and went back to the store and fetched the new duds Job had purchased. Thirty minutes later Job was back out front and starving to death. Something about bathing makes a feller hungry and Job was ready to eat.

Supper was spread on a large table at the back of the store and everyone gathered to find a seat. Mr. Johnson had Job a seat next to him and Angie across the table beside Mrs. Johnson. Before they could be seated, Job asked to do something important. He fetched the fancy pinafore from the counter and handed it to Mrs. Johnson, saying, "I think this is meant to keep you from soiling that pretty blue dress. Anyway, I want Angie to have it as a present."

Angie buried her face in her hands crying and Job felt like a fool. He had a questionable look on his face.

Mr. Johnson leaned over and whispered, "It's a woman thang, Job, believe me, she loves it."

Sure enough, Angie quickly dried her eyes, ran around the table and planted a kiss on Job's cheek. Mrs. Johnson helped her slip the garment on and they all took their places laughing and talking. The boys, John and James, were enjoying this change of routine around the store and Mrs. Johnson had to corral them. Job was afraid to look at Angie after the show of affection he received. He never in his life had experienced a kiss from a woman in public, and a pretty white girl to boot! He was too hungry to worry about it now so he would figure it all out later.

Mr. Johnson called everybody to silence and offered a prayer of thanks for the food and safe return of Angie and for their new friend and hero, Job. Mr. Johnson had a little serving system for the big table and he picked up the biscuit plate, took one and passed it clockwise to Job. He continued with all the other vittles till all were served. There were field peas, turnip greens, candied yams, stewed potatoes with onions and fried cotton tail rabbit. Just out of reach, Job noticed a bread pudding cooling off.

Everyone was chowin' down and bragging on the cook when little James looked at Job and asked, "Are you really a real Injun?"

There was a sudden pause and silence to the table but Job never stopped sopping pea juice and replied, "I sure am James. My mother was a Cherokee Indian from one of the seven clans of Georgia. Both my daddy and grandpa married Cherokee women.

"Yore daddy was white, huh?" James continued.

Job could tell folks was a little uncomfortable with the conversation because you never know what a nine year old will ask next. He pressed on to help the child understand. His daddy had said that ignorance was the greatest enemy of the American Indian and to always take the opportunity to inform folks.

"Yep. My grandpa was white too. That makes me half white and half Indian." Job smiled at James and John.

"A half breed! That's what people call you when they come by the store!" John interjected wanting to show his knowledge of the subject.

Mr. Johnson jumped in quickly, "John, James, that's enough! Don't be saying that word around this house anymore!" Both boys went back to fiddlin' with their grub.

Job decided best not to stir the issue and just smiled at Mr. Johnson and winked. Everyone laughed and began passing the food again.

Mrs. Johnson was serving the bread pudding herself, not chancing on the boys helping themselves. The pudding was divine and Job said so as much.

"Ya'll eat bread puddin' in Georgia?" Mrs. Johnson asked.

"Yes, Mam, but I don't believe I ever et none as good as this!" Job said.

"My Lord! I just throwed it together from scratch." She said beaming.

"Well this scratch just took care of my itch!" Job remarked, and everyone laughed.

Supper was finished, the women folk took over the kitchen, the boys beat it outside and Mr. Johnson and Job walked out to the front porch. Job was not sure what to do next. Mr. Johnson began to tell him what he would like to do next morning.

"Job, if you and Angie is up to it, I would like to get a early start in the morning and deliver her to her family." He offered.

"You mean you comin' along?" Job asked.

"Yes, matter of fact; I'm bringin the whole family. I wouldn't miss this reunion for love or money. Folks spent days and weeks frettin' and lookin' for that girl. I plan on being there for the ending." He finished chuckling.

"That sounds good to me." Job replied. He was happy to be part of something this good.

"I'll let the family and Angie know that we'll be headin out at first light." Mr. Johnson finished saying and slapped Job on the back before walking back into the kitchen.

Job heard the ladies rejoicing. All of a sudden John and James cut loose yelling when they heard the news. They probably never been over two miles from home Job thought as he went about tending to the mule. Mrs. Johnson had made him a pallet in the store and not long after sundown everyone was asleep.

CHAPTER 9

HOME COMING!

The next morning Job was already out and about when he heard the Johnson's rousing the boys from bed. He had taken care of the mule and packed everything into the new saddle bags. With extra clothes he still had extra room in the bags. He was glad to have a safe, dry place for the family Bible. His birth certificate and family history was all in the book. He was kicking around out front when Mrs. Johnson called him to come in for coffee and breakfast. She was frying salt pork and setting the table with cold biscuits and cane syrup. Job begged her out of another bite of the bread pudding with his coffee and from then on she hovered around him like a settin' hen catering to his every need. Everyone was entertained with her spoiling Job. It was especially amusing to Angie because she saw how much he liked being spoiled so she pitched in a little attention. She had got a little buzz from the peck on the cheek that she gave him last night. Now she was real curious about what he might have felt.

Mr. Johnson had the freight wagon harnessed with two horses and his saddle horse tied behind. There were blankets and left over vittles packed inside. Mr. Johnson was anticipating a celebration and brought along his fiddle. He had locked the store and left a note on the shingle out front. It read, "Angie Cooper rescued! Git together at Cooper farm. Be back tomorrow. Hep yourself to water." B. Johnson.

Job rode out in front of the wagon to avoid the dust. The boys, James and John, had snuggled down into the blankets and were asleep. Mr. and

Mrs. Johnson took up the wagon seat and Angie was leaned up behind them keeping warm in the cold morning air. The Cooper farm was about ten miles further down to the trail west. They were making good time and Job figured at this pace they would cover ten miles before noon. About an hour out, they met a lone rider, a mail dispatcher. Mr. Johnson hailed him in and explained what was going on and took the mail that was posted for his store. He then dispatched a note to the constable in B'ham with the news of Angie's rescue. He asked the mail carrier to spread the word of her rescue and the feller lit out like a bat out a hell! The news he was carrying would set the pulpits on fire and make for some good gossipin' for weeks to come!

The day turned out fair and the travelers talked back and forth to break the monotony of the journey. Job tried to sneak a glimpse of Angie when he could and she seemed to be lookin' his way every time. Something about this girl bothered him. It wasn't a bad bother but he just didn't know what to do or say around her anymore. Maybe he was just overprotective of her till he could get her home. He would settle for that conclusion.

Angie's' anticipation and excitement was obvious to everyone. Every mile seemed to add to her joy and expectation of arriving home. She leaned out of the wagon and told Job they were not over two hours away from her home. She was now perched on the sideboards taking in the familiar countryside with tear filled eyes. John and James were awake and they were probing her with questions about her family and what she had seen in B'ham. It was a noisy little group moving along the trail.

Mr. Johnson pulled up to a natural artesian spring beside the road and they all rinsed off and enjoyed a picnic of the leftovers from last night's supper. The spring looked like a regular stop for travelers because of the worn spot around the spring. There were initials carved in a huge sycamore shade tree. Sure enough, a rider appeared out of nowhere from an old trail leading in from the north. Mr. Johnson gave the rider the same information he had given to the mail carrier, then he turned and rode back north the way he came. The feller had a hunting dog missing and was out looking for the animal. He said he would spread the news back toward his place.

After everyone was refreshed and full of leftovers, they loaded the wagon and took to the trail again. Being as close to home, Angie was all to pieces with excitement. Her face was streaked with tear tracks and dust. Job took a glance often and he could not fathom how another human being could mistreat such an innocent and beautiful person. Job noticed that Mrs. Johnson had wet a rag from the water keg and was primping the girl to see her folks. Job wondered just how this was gonna pan out. Those poor folks are believin' that their only child was dead. Matter of fact they had buried her in a memorial service. This could be a load on that mama's heart. He would hope for the best and he prepared for the worst.

Thirty minutes later Mr. Johnson said they were a quarter of a mile out. He then did something that was also common back in Georgia. He halted the wagon, stood to his feet and let out a hog call you could hear for three miles. Job listened as it reverberated through the hollers. There was a minute pause and he repeated the call. An arrival announcement like this carried several meanings. Someone was bringing either good or bad news or they just didn't want to surprise anyone and get shot trespassing.

A good three minutes had passed and a little northwest of the trail a long high pitched yodel came drifting back.

Angie went berserk, crying, "Its daddy's voice! That's his call!"

Everybody was all smiles watching her face beaming with joy. Mr. Johnson reined the horses ahead and they dropped over a rise into a large meadow that stretched for half a mile north of the trail. There was a grove of red oak and hickory trees almost in the center of the clearing. A nice looking boxing farmhouse was tucked beneath the shade trees. There were cross fences and a hog pen at the southwest corner next to a creek. Northwest of the house was a tater field that was being turned. Job could see a middle aged man propped up on a turning plow hitched behind a large mule. Red even perked up at the scent of his own kind. The man had set his plow waiting on the travelers to come into the clearing.

Mr. Johnson stopped his wagon, set the brake and turned to Angie.

"Angie, I need to ride in and get your folks ready to see you. They have been through hell and a surprise like this could kill your mama. She had some kind of breakdown and we just need to be careful." He asked Angie to be patient.

"That's fine Mr. Johnson. Just wave when you want me to come in." She agreed.

Turning to the boys he quipped, "You boys behave. I'll be right back."

"Yes sir, yes sir" like two parrots they replied.

Unhitching his horse from the rear of the wagon, Mr. Johnson turned to Job and said, "Job, ride along with me."

They crossed the meadow, passed the house and rode to the tater field where Mr. Cooper stood watching everyone.

The men all hollered at one another as they rode up to the plow mule. Red's ears were forward and he was blowing something fierce. Job patted and consoled him and he calmed down a bit.

"What you say neighbor! It ain't Christmas, what you doing way out here Mr. Johnson?" Ely Cooper grinned reaching out to shake hands.

"It's good news, Mr. Cooper. This here's Job Irvin from Georgia. He's passin' through on his way to Texas. We brought you some good news about Angie."

Mr. Cooper dropped the reins to his mule and his countenance turned ashen. "They found her? Did somebody find her body?" He begged with his eyes.

"Yes sir! They found her, this here feller found her, Mr. Cooper . . . and she's alive!"

Job had never seen such an incredulous look. Mr. Cooper tried to speak but couldn't, his legs went out from under him and he collapsed to his knees in the fresh turned dirt. He just knelt there sobbing and staring at both men.

"Where, where's my baby?" He finally got the words out as they helped him to his feet.

"Alive? Ben, we buried her! How you know it's her? Who's got her, Injuns?" Mr. Cooper was desperate for an explanation.

Ben Johnson was bursting to tell this father that his daughter was in the wagon and knew only one way to break the news. There was no easy way to conclude the matter.

Ben Johnson laid a hand on each shoulder of Mr. Cooper, looked him dead in the eye and with trembling lips said, "Coop, Angie's in my wagon right yonder and she's just fine!"

Mr. Cooper gazed past Job and Ben for a full minute trying to comprehend what he was hearing. Here he was standing in a dirty tater field only a shell of a man three minutes ago. Now he was receiving the best news of his life, the news that was already reviving his spirit and the only thing that would ever resurrect his tormented and broken hearted wife.

Mr. Cooper was about to break away for the wagon when Ben said, "Coop, what about Ellen? Can she handle this? Where is she?" He scanned the house for any sign of her.

"She's holed up in her room, Ben. She hardly ever gets out anymore." Mr. Cooper stated.

"Let's be careful and take it a step at a time. Let's get Angie in here to you and we will go from there." Ben continued, then lifted his arm and gave a wave at the wagon. Mrs. Johnson reined the horses and wagon into the meadow leading to the house. Mr. Cooper had already began to double time toward the trail. The wagon was just not fast enough for Angie when she saw her daddy coming that way. Like a rabbit she leaped from the wagon and ran lickety split down the trail. That's all the boys, John and James needed, was an excuse to break free from the wagon. Like two beagles after a rabbit, they were right behind her.

Mr. Cooper had broke into a full run when he saw Angie leap from the wagon. They covered the hundred yards fast as any horse Job had ever seen run. The moment everyone had waited for was here! Job thought he wouldn't trade what he was witnessing for a fortune in gold. He felt such satisfaction in having a part in this family reunion.

The two were still hugging and crying as everyone else reached the spot. They finally released one another and Angie went about hugging everyone gathered. She was beside herself with joy and tears. Mr. Cooper was shaking everyone's hands over again.

Job had never dismounted and Angie walked up to the mule, looked up at him and said, "Git down here Job Irvin!" He shook his head grinning and eased off the mule not knowing what to expect. Angie reached up and wrapped her arms around his neck, pulling his face down, she looked him in the eye and said, "Thank you, Job!" and planted a soft, hot kiss square on his lips! Job just froze and turned deep red. The young boys began hopping and hollering when they saw what happened and that made Job feel even more embarrassed. Everyone laughed and things began to settle down a bit.

Mr. Johnson broke in to say, "Ely, maybe it'd be better if you and Martha broke the news to Ellen. We'll be right there if you need us."

"You're right, Ben. Let's do it! I believe I'm fixin' to git my wife back from the dead today, too!" Hope was transforming the man as he spoke. He already looked ten years younger since they arrived, thought Job.

Everyone moved to the front porch of the farmhouse. Mr. Cooper and Martha went inside and everyone quieted down to try and hear what was being said.

Mr. and Mrs. Cooper's bedroom was on the southwest corner of the house to take advantage of the sun's warmth in winter. Mr. Cooper stopped at the closed door and called out, "Ellen, you awake? You got compnee!" He opened the door a little and said, "I'm comin in and Ellen Johnson wants to see you, she's comin in with me."

Martha heard Ellen reply, "My Lord, Coop! Not like this, I'm a mess!"

"We'll give you a minute to cover up." He responded as he pulled the door closed.

They could hear Ellen moving around the room and a minute later she invited them inside. Ely eased the door open and they stepped into the stuffy bedroom. The chamber pot needed emptying for the smell of urine was strong. Ellen was sitting in a rocking chair and Martha could not recognize the vibrant and beautiful woman she had seen only months ago. Ellen Cooper was skin and bones. There were black circles around her eyes and from her skin color, she must not have been outside in weeks.

"What a surprise, Martha. You're a sight for sore eyes." She said in a weak voice.

"Hello, Ellen." Martha said as she moved to her side to give her a hug. Martha was weeping profusely and Ellen was confused at the tears. She looked at Coop with inquisitive eyes and saw that he too was weeping.

Holding Martha at arms length, Ellen asked, "What is it Martha! What's wrong?" She questioned.

"Nothings wrong Ellen." Martha's smile beamed through the hot tears.

"We come to tell you something good Ellen!" she said squeezing her hands.

Ellen cast a desperate glance at her husband.

"It's about Angie? They found her body?" Ellen pleaded for an answer.

Ely knelt before Ellen taking her face in his hands and said, "It's about Angie, Ellen. They found her alright . . . Ellen . . . she's not dead, she's alive and well!"

Ellen never moved or winced. She sat staring at Coop but not seeing him. Perhaps she saw her only child or felt her in her womb or nursing again at her breast. She sat for the longest and finally a large single tear began slowly down her cheek. With it another followed carrying months of anguish, heartbreak, fear and torment with them. Martha could see life seeping back into her countenance. Ellen turned from Ely and looked at Martha with the greatest hunger for more good news about her lost daughter. She then squeezed Martha's hands till they began to hurt. She asked her, pleadingly, "Tell me, Martha, tell me the truth. Don't be afraid, I only want the truth."

Martha glanced at Coop for consent to go any further and he nodded and smiled.

"Ellen, there's nothing to be afraid of anymore. Believe me, Angie is alive . . . and well . . . she is alive Ellen!"

"My baby, where is she?" She whispered like she was afraid to let the moment go or maybe wake up from a dream.

Taking Ellen close to her, Martha asked Ellen soberly, "Will you promise to breathe deeply and stay with us if I tell you?" Martha implored.

"Yes. Why? What are you trying to say?" She asked glancing back and forth from Martha to Ely.

"Ellen, Angie is alive and well. She's O.K . . . Ellen . . . Angie is here, on the porch, on your porch Ellen!" Martha said with joy.

Job had never heard anything like the sound from the house. It wasn't a wail or a scream but more like a release of the deepest frustrations and anguish. They heard shuffling inside and it was too much for Angie. She opened the front door and stepped into the living room. The others followed not knowing what to expect. The bedroom door opened wide and Ely stepped through followed by Martha who was supporting Ellen as they entered the room. No one would ever forget the joy and relief that they saw on Ellen's face that day. Like wind beneath a bird's wings, she left Martha's side and fell into Angie's embrace. There wasn't a dry eye in the house. Even the boys were sniffling and trying to conceal their tears.

An hour later, Mrs. Cooper was still holding her daughter. She wouldn't let her out of her sight. She asked if they could move their chairs outside in the afternoon sun. Naturally, Ely invited everyone to spend the night and Ben Johnson agreed and asked that Martha be allowed to take over the kitchen. Coop agreed and Martha began to organize a big supper to celebrate. Ben had figured that when word got out about Angie, folks would be gathering at the Cooper farm immediately. He was right, for before long, wagons and riders began coming in from every direction. Job counted six families gathered in the yard. In these parts when someone died, got married or had a baby, folks would come bringing food to prepare and their bedding to spend the night, so they could stay and celebrate.

Ely and the men built up a big fire and broke out the poppin' corn and dried peanuts from the crib. The ladies were all hovered around Ellen and Angie catching up on news. The kids were playing marbles and hop scotch in the yard. This is all good and he was glad to be part of it and alive, thought Job.

CHAPTER 10

HEAD OVER HEELS IN LOVE!

Folks had continued to drop by the Cooper farm all evening for a visit and a drink of water. Another family had pulled in and was spending the night. Martha Johnson and the womenfolk had whipped up a mulligan stew with cornbread to feed everyone. Ben Johnson had broke out his fiddle and was tuning it up. A banjo was plucking away and one feller was blowing on a jug. A teenage boy was stroking a rub board with a chicken bone.

Most folks now knew the story of how Job had rescued Angie and he felt like an Atlanta politician, his hand had been shook so many times. The fact he was Cherokee didn't have to be advertised. Even though he had risked his life for Angie, the prejudice was evident in the way he was shunned. Most whites would never mistreat or be hostile to an Indian but tradition and their raising kept them from association with color. Most folks would treat him as an equal in private but in the public eye they would pull away. The Indian Removal Act of 1830 and the Trail of Tears incident had only reinforced the prejudice. The American Indian was made to feel like a foreigner in their ancestral land. Job could only pity the ignorance and suffer the injustice till folks were educated to see the truth.

As late evening approached, the music got together and a regular hoe down began. Job didn't dare approach a white girl to dance but enjoyed watching the show. The children had their own dance circle and were acting silly. Angie was the center of attraction and Job couldn't figure where she got all that energy. She kept watching him and it bothered him but not in an unpleasant way.

Finally, the music slowed to a southern waltz and Job was caught off guard when Angie appeared in front of him with both hands extended in an invitation to dance. Job was embarrassed because he had never danced and it might not set right with the local customs.

Angie wouldn't back down and finally he took her hands and she led off in a slow waltz.

"You just follow me," she instructed realizing his limitations.

He stumbled along with her till he got the rhythm and was beginning to feel better. She had moved in closer to him for comfort and went to talking.

"Lest I don't get a chance, I want to thank you again for what all you've done for me and my family. I feel indebted to you," she said sweetly and Job felt warm inside just listening.

"You plumb welcome, Miss Cooper, but let's not have to do it again," he said light heartedly, trying to avoid the intimacy he felt he wanted with this woman. He had seen his mother look at his daddy the way Angie was looking at him now and it shook him up real bad. He knew there was more than just a feeling of indebtedness in those eyes for he hoped he would never have to let her go.

"Maybe we could talk later, before I have to go," he wanted her to know he enjoyed her company.

What he said sent a streak of hurt and surprise in her eyes and she replied, "Go! Job, we just got here. You need to rest up and I want you to meet my folks. They don't know you like they should. You're special to this family now and especially to me!" She squeezed his hands and pleaded with her eyes for assurance.

"I'll hang around a couple a days, just for you," he surprised himself by what he heard come out of his mouth. He didn't know if his head was doing the talking or his heart. Anyway, it worked, for Angie was all tear filled eyes and smiles. Job was more light footed and closer than ever when the waltz ended. He knew it was time for a cold drink of water and some fresh air! Pop had warned him that the right woman would make you drunk without the spirits. Well, Job felt dizzy and he needed to sober up fast. He made his way to the water well and rinsed his face with the cold water. He had finished a dipper of water when Mr. Cooper strolled up to the well.

"Job, I know I've told you a dozen times today that I appreciate you but I just want to say it again. You helped give me my life back and I feel I owe you," he stated plainly.

"No sir, Mr. Cooper, nobody owes me anything. I just done what any decent God fearing man would do. My life is richer having met all you folks. Maybe someday I can drop back by for a visit." Job said.

"That's why I want to talk with you before you make plans. Angie has told me about Texas and your pioneering spirit. I'd like to spend some time with you and hear more about Texas after this crowd clears out tomorrow. Maybe you could stick around a couple of days and rest your mule," he offered, grinning.

Job knew Angie had done her homework and it amused him.

"I'd like that, Mr. Cooper. A couple of days won't hurt nothing," he answered.

Mr. Cooper perked up and said, "It's settled then, I'm going to tell the missus and she'll be happy 'bout that." He took a dipper of water, drank it and moved off toward his wife. Job noticed Angie had been watching all this time and he saw her daddy nod his head at her and she burst into the biggest smile of the evening. This was one conniving female but he was learning to like her more by the minute.

All but the overnighters had cleared out and everyone was picking out a place to bed down. The front porch and living room accommodated most of the folks so Job settled in the barrel house or tater kiln where the taters were kept dry. There was a sorting table under cover and he spread his bedroll on top of the table and walked back to the fire where the men were talking while finishing off the roasted peanuts. Job was glad he was not sleeping inside with this bunch after all the popcorn and peanuts they had eaten.

Ben Johnson had the floor when Job walked up and as usual the conversation was about slavery, the Presidential elections and Texas.

Ben was finishing his statement, "We can't allow no Yankee president or federal government to come into Alabama and tell us how to run our lives. I'll pull up and move to Texas before that happens!" There were several nods and grunts in agreement as he finished. Job found a hickory block and perched atop it and commenced to stoking the fire. One feller was carving a chew from a plug of tobacco and he passed it over to Job. Job took the plug, slid the skinning knife from his boot sleeve and sliced a nice chew before passing it to the next man. He noticed everyone eyeballing the skinning knife as he cleaned it well before sheathing the blade. The tobacco was a little sweeter than he was used to but it was worth putting in your mouth. He nodded at the feller that shared the chew and said, "Mighty fine blend."

The old feller looked pleased and said, "Wild honey, most folks use cane syrup but I lean heavy on wild honey. Took me a long time to git it right but it was worth my time. Thank ye."

A mule skinner across the fire said he had tried rum flavored tobacco in New Orleans and nearly puked his guts out. Everyone laughed and the stories got bigger and better till everyone got tired and sat listening to the night sounds. One old man got up and walked to the edge of the firelight and farted like a bay mule. The men roared with laughter.

The men had forgotten that the ladies had moved to the front porch to gossip and one of them cried out, "John Henry! Don't you bring none of that filth to my bed. You can sleep out there with the dogs!" she said teasingly. The lady folks burst into laughter and the men likewise.

Ben Johnson changed the subject and let everyone know he would be leaving for the store before noon the next day. He went on to tell of a catalog from upstate from which he could order just about anything they would need on the farm, even a mail order bride! The catalog had pictures of harnesses, furniture and kitchen stoves. He could get a turning plow in thirty days from the day he posted the order! They all began to carry on about how modern and crowded their neck of the woods had become. One local said he had a new neighbor that had moved within six miles of his place and the others sympathized with the crowded conditions. Job chuckled to himself, thinking of the half dozen plumes of chimney smoke he could see from the old place in Georgia. These folks had some surprises coming as the big towns were popping up on the trails west.

As the fire burned down the last time, the men broke away to their beds. Job said goodnight and retired to his pallet. For the next hour he could hear the men and women drawing water to rinse off before bedding down. The water must be ice cold, for he could hear giggles and sighs as people took their coon baths. The full day caught up with him and Job slipped into the best sleep he'd had in a long time. Something had given him rest in his mind and spirit. Was it the fun filled evening or the beautiful girl he had danced with that left him at ease? It must have been the well water he drank with the peanuts, he mused to himself and that's all he remembered till daylight.

It was all hustle and bustle the next morning as folks packed up to leave for home. Mrs. Johnson had baked about fifty cat head biscuits and heated up what was left of the mulligan stew. There was a gallon of coffee already simmering at the fire outside. Job grabbed two of the cat head biscuits and poured a cup of the hot coffee. He decided to walk out to the tater field where it was quiet and he could make some plans. He had never seen taters raised on a commercial scale and thought he might pick up an idea or two for later on down the road in life. There was a barrel house where the harvested potatoes were kept dry and crated or put in barrels for shipping to town. The sorting table was big and heavy but low enough to back a wagon up to it and offload the potatoes by hand. He was lost in thought when Ben Johnson walked up with a "Good morning." They exchanged pleasantries and Mr. Johnson handed Job a letter to the sheriff in Tuscaloosa with instructions for the reward.

"Don't feel bad about taking the money, Job. We paid the taxes and we want you to have the reward." Ben said pointedly.

"I appreciate it and Lord knows I can use it." Job replied.

They walked back to the wagon together and Ben shook Job's hand and said, "You got a place to hang yer hat if you ever back though here." Ben climbed on to the wagon with his wife and kids.

Job looked up at Martha and said, "If Mrs. Johnson will stir up another bread puddin' I'll make it a point to drop in soon!"

Martha beamed with surprise and said, "Honey, I'll keep the oven hot!" and let out in one of her belly laughs. Everyone laughed and waved as they pulled away back up the trail east.

The Cooper family was seeing everyone off and Job sidled up next to Angie and said, "Good mornin'." She replied the same and gave him that smile he felt he might kill for. She was wearing a different color dress today but the same pinafore he had bought for her. He caught himself staring and decided he best walk back out to the tater shed and scout around a bit. A little later Mr. Cooper joined him and began to point out his operation and how it worked. He said he was breaking up the tater field to get ready for the February planting season. Job let him know that he had some plowing experience and asked if he could help. Ely was more than glad to share that burden. He helped Job get familiar with the plow mule and pointed out the depth he was aiming for then let him go. It took Job a full turn to get his rhythm or speed but the plow cut like a knife through butter as he got the plow depth correct. Ely was well pleased and went to work on the other chores that he had got behind on lately.

An hour later, Job had broke a sweat following the plow. He set the plow and walked to the well for a cool drink of water. Ely kept a bucket of drinking water drawn so Job dipped and drank until he got the water belly. Ellen Cooper came out for a bucket of cooking water and Job drew a bucket for her. She was back in her kitchen and said dinner would be ready at noon.

As Job turned to go back to the field she said, "Job, we're so happy you could stay a while. I don't know what to say 'cept I honestly believe the Hand of God is in this. I was defeated Job, and I was draggin' Coop down with me. You came along just in time. I'm forever grateful." She finished as a tear coursed down her face and turned back toward the house. Job returned to plowing for another hour and a half while mulling over his mixed emotions and when to take up the trail again. He was past due for a rest when he caught sight of Angie waving him in for dinner. He unlatched the plow and led the mule to the water trough. Angie had the wash bucket and soap ready as he and Ely walked up.

"Why, ain't this nice. You'd think we had compnee', wouldn't you Job?" Ely remarked winking at Job. Job grinned back and noticed Angie had blushed a little at her daddy's picking. She went back to the kitchen door never saying a word. The men dried off and Ely led Job into the kitchen. Now Job liked this. There was a real table cloth on the dining table. Job hardly ever seen a fork and one was laid out beside each spoon. There was also a cloth napkin the same color of the table cloth beside each plate. Job had never seen plates as pretty as these. He was getting a little bit nervous on how to approach all this fancy stuff.

Ely seated Job next to him and the women found their places. Ely bowed his head for grace and everyone did the same.

"We use this fine Chiny for special occasions, and Ellen wanted to honor you with this dinner, Job." He looked at Ellen with a pleasing smile. Ellen was fidgeting with her napkin till the attention passed.

"This is all nice and purty and I appreciate it," Job said sincerely.

Mrs. Cooper had prepared a venison roast with Irish potatoes and had cooked it down to a rich, brown gravy. There was hominy and a fresh baked apple pie. The only sounds to be heard was smacking and a few grunts occasionally.

Ellen passed Job the biscuits and remarked, "Angie told me she had never met such a well mannered man as you, Job. You must come from a good family in Georgee."

"Yes Mam, they were the best, lost everyone to the smallpox and measles. Just me and my grandpa survived and now he lives on the coast in Savannah." Job replied kindly, keeping it brief.

"Well, I know the Lord will work things out for such a kind hearted man like you. Lord knows we need decency in these neck of the woods," she added.

Changing the subject, Ely broke in and said, "There's a few winter huckleberries left to pick on the tree line in the northwest corner of the tater field. Angie offered to pick 'em, but not alone. Job, why don't you take it easy after dinner and hep her out?"

"That's fine with me but pickin' huckleberries is not my favorite chore." Job informed everyone that he understood the tedious job ahead. Everyone laughed in agreement.

Dinner was over and Job waited by the well till the ladies cleaned up the kitchen. Angie soon came out carrying two wooden bowls and they took out across the field to the tree line. The bushes had barely enough berries left to make a cobbler. They were real seedy and the purple juice would be squeezed from the berry and be used in the cobbler. They scoured the bushes in less than an hour and finally settled on an old log in sight of the farmhouse. Job was lost for conversation but Angie took up the slack.

"What are your plans for leaving, Job?" Angie inquired. "I don't want you to just pop up and leave on a dime." she smiled at him inviting a clue of what to expect.

"I was hoping to light out at daybreak Monday morning," Job stated as he fished around in the bowl sorting out the wormy berries.

"That'll give me the rest of the day to hep your daddy with the rest of the plowin' and I can visit with you all day Sunday." He nervously looked at her as he finished.

"Why Job Irvin, you mean to say you're gonna come callin' on Sunday?" she teased him laughing out loud.

He laughed with her but when his eyes met hers, something came over him and he said flat out, "Angie, if things were different and I lived close by, yore daddy would have to run me off! I've never had a girlfriend but if I did it would have to be you." Job didn't know things would get so mushy so fast but he was glad he said what he felt. Angie had flushed red as a berry and tears filled her eyes as she reached and took his berry stained hands. There was a silence that seemed like forever and she finally spoke.

"Job, look at me. I've had crushes on boys. I've been almost soiled by that kidnapper. Seems like I've felt every emotion the heart could know. But one thing I know deep in my soul is that I don't want to live this life without you. I know you got the itch to see Texas. I want you to know that I will never leave this farm or see another man till you come back after me. I mean it Job! I love you Job Irvin, and I believe you feel the same way for me. I'll be here till I hear from you and I will come to wherever you are, when you need me."

Job wished he had words like that but all he could say was, "I love you Angie. My mother said I would find a soul mate in life and you are that woman, Angie Cooper!" Job squeezed her hand and rose from the log and helped her up to return home. They crossed the field hand in hand and Job could see Mrs. Cooper watching from the well. He was positive he saw her smile as she watched the two of them hand in hand. Job didn't mind what anyone would think about his feelings for Angie. This was meant to be, it was right and it was settled. Angie didn't know it yet but he was going to Texas to build a home and she was to be his wife. He had never felt so positive or encouraged about anything before. Suddenly everything took on a new meaning and Angie glanced at his face noticing the fire and joy burning there.

Job plowed the rest of the evening and they had an early supper of leftovers. Job informed Mr. and Mrs. Cooper of his plans to leave early Monday morning. They told him to sleep late Sunday and they would all observe the Sabbath together.

The next day was cold and blustery. After a breakfast of fried taters, biscuits and gravy, Coop broke out the family Bible and led them all in devotion.

The day flew by and that evening, they were eating the last of the huckleberry cobbler when Job surprised them all by saying, "Mr. and Mrs. Cooper, while I'm out in Texas, I'd like permission to correspond with Angie. And some day in the near future I would like to come callin' on her." Job could see Ellen was pleased by what she heard and Angie was flushed red and fiddlin' with her fork.

Mr. Cooper seemed to be lost in thought. Taking the last sip of coffee, he spoke, "Job, you already seem like one of our own. You feel plumb welcome to write and come callin' when you get ready. Matter of fact, when you write, tell us about Texas. If it sounds good enough, we may just move out there! It's getting' awful crowded here." Everyone was relieved to be in agreement. Job felt one step closer to his destiny.

Everyone retired early. Job packed his saddle bags and checked out the mule and saddle. He filled his canteen and went to bed a happy and blessed man just thinking about his future with Angie and TEXAS!

CHAPTER 11

REWARD

There was a cold north wind blowing the next morning and it felt like a rain in the air. Job saddled Red and packed his gear. Seeing the coal oil lamp on in the kitchen, he went inside. Mrs. Cooper was frying eggs and salt pork. The biscuits were out and coffee steaming on the stove. Ely walked in and sat down with Job at the table. Mrs. Cooper began to serve the breakfast. Job noticed Angie was running late. The next moment she walked in and over her blue dress she was wearing the fancy pinafore he had bought for her. She sat down in the lamp light and Job could feel his heart thump as her red hair gleamed in the lamp light. Her eyes were red like she had been crying and a pain hit him suddenly as he realized he was about to ride off and leave her. Man, let's get this over with, he thought to himself. After exchanging pleasantries, they all ate in silence. Mrs. Cooper had packed a gunny sack with leftover biscuits, salt pork and a jar of wild honey. She had written their names on a script and handed this to Job. He put this with his Bible. Everyone followed Job out to his mule. It was a grey daylight now and cold with a falling mist. Mr. and Mrs. Cooper both hugged his neck and Ellen went to sobbing. They turned back into the house leaving Angie and Job alone.

Angie couldn't bring herself to look up into Job's face so he took her face in both hands. Looking deeply into her green eyes he whispered, "Angie, listen to me! I love you and I will be back. You make plans to be with me. Don't give up, write when you can and I'll do the same." Angie was trembling and hot tears were streaming down her face.

Reaching up and feeling of his face and eyes she whispered, "Job, don't wait too long. Things don't have to be perfect for me. If you can't come back this way, send for me, I'll come anywhere you are. I love you, Job Irvin."

Having never released her face in his hands, Job leaned down and placed his lips over hers. The universe seemed to explode as they fell into each others arms. They kissed for minutes and stood hugging one another in the cold misty morning. Job knew he'd never leave if this kept up any longer. He could see spending his life with this woman and he was gonna get things right so he could take care of her. One last time he pressed into her hot lips. Their "I love you's" filled the air as he turned and mounted the mule. He reined the mule toward the trail west turning a half dozen times to wave before disappearing into the tree line. Angie stood for the longest in the yard. She sent a prayer after him for his safe and soon return. Ely and Ellen observed their beautiful daughter grieving in the yard but content knowing they were gaining the best son-in-law in shoe leather!

Ely had told Job he was less than three hours from Tuscaloosa. He pressed on in the cold hoping to find the sheriff and take care of the reward money today. Even though he had the official letter from Ben Johnson, he was leary of dealing with strangers about money, especially when it was about a white girl being kidnapped. If push come to shove, he would high tail it out of there. He wasn't waiting around for no mail carriers or investigations. Sure enough, two hours into the ride the farms and shacks got more plentiful. The blue smoke from the chimneys and smoke houses lay low and heavy over the road. There wasn't very much traffic in the cold morning.

He noticed a clap board sign nailed to a tree that read Tuscaloosa, Alabama and saw a neat row of single story buildings ahead. Continuing along the trail he searched for the sheriff's office or jail. Passing through to the west end of town he came upon a brick building with bars in the windows and a sign saying, Sheriff, painted on a post. There was blue smoke rising from the stove pipe so someone was inside the jail. Job half hitched Red to a tie post, shook himself off a little to look half decent then lifted the iron latch on the door. He stepped inside a very warm open room and noticed the cell was a forged iron cage that took up one corner. The pot belly stove was in the south corner next to the road. A chair and table sat next to the stove and a middle aged pot bellied man with a tin star sat shuffling papers at the table. A pot of coffee had boiled and the burnt aroma filled the room.

Job removed his hat and nodded to the sheriff as he spoke, "Mornin' Sheriff", he offered.

The sheriff with a quizzical look nodded and replied, "Mornin' stranger, what can I do for you?"

Job stepped to the table while fishing for the letter from Ben Johnson out of his shirt pocket and passed it to the sheriff. The sheriff picked up a pair of reading spectacles then scanned the letter. His eyebrows worked up and down as he read like he was trying to imagine what events took place behind the letter. Job was turning in front of the stove trying to dry out and warm his hands.

The sheriff finished reading the letter and looking at Job said, "That's the best news I've heard since Christmas, Mister! I know the puke you collared and believe me I want to git my hands on that scum," he scowled glaring at the letter.

"What's your name and where you from, son?" the sheriff inquired..

"Job Irvin. I was raised just outside of Atlanta, Georgia. Pox and measles took my family so I'm moving out to Texas," he offered.

"Hmm," the sheriff mused, "Pox hard on Injuns, they tell me." He carefully probed to see if his profile of Job was correct.

Job got the point and responded directly, "Yes sir, Cherokee. Mother and grandmother were bloods," he offered.

"Well, this all looks in order but I can't get the reward money till the bank opens at 9 o'clock. In the meantime, don't wander off cause they's folks around here still thinks it's open season on Injuns," he quipped with a half grin.

"Hep yerself to the coffee and I'll go see what I can get done. If the clerk is in early he'll take care of the matter for me," he remarked as he picked up the letter and his hat and left the building.

Job walked back out to the mule to retrieve his drinking cup for the coffee. He would be extra careful what he put to his lips after his brush with food poisoning. Having poured a swallow of coffee, he looked over the reward posters tacked on the wall. This must be outlaw country, he mused, as he scanned the dozen wanted posters. Low and behold, there was the poster seeking information on Angie Cooper and someone had sketched a remarkable likeness to her. Job reached up and tenderly removed the poster and folding it one time around the sketch, he slid it inside his shirt. The likeness of her on the poster moved him to a sudden warmth all over.

Thirty minutes later the sheriff was stomping back inside and looked well pleased for his troubles. He laid out a warrant for Job to sign that would accompany Angie's signature and counted out $42.00, the remainder of the reward minus the pinafore and dry goods.

"I'd advise you to ride on out of Tuscaloosee 'bout eight miles before you stop again. They's a mercantile out that way an they'll take anybody's money. Another thang, I wouldn't travel alone past the mercantile if you value yore hide. Find somebody goin' that way and jine 'em. They's some scally wags on that road west and the more with you, the safer you'll be!" he advised Job.

Picking up the money and the letting the sheriff know he took Angie's wanted poster, Job thanked the sheriff and left the office. The day was looking a little drier and Job's spirits picked up as he mounted Red. He knew the news of the reward money was already out and he wanted to get well ahead of the gossip, if he could, before dark. Forty two dollars was killing money in these parts. Sure enough, several loafers watched him enviously as he rode through town. He laid his hand on the pistol butt to convince the gainsayers he would tolerate no foolishness. Having made his exit, Job clicked the mule into a fair gait to get some distance from Tuscaloosee before sundown.

Ely had told Job that the Mississippi line would be 3-4 days ride from Tuscaloosa but he had been no further. Maybe a day's ride into Ol' Miss there was a boomin' town called Meridian. Job decided to push on till dark thirty unless he came upon a good stream of water. He found himself patting the poster of Angie in his shirt and took it out for another look. A man would have to either be crazy for ridin' away from a darlin' like Angie or else have a sure enough proposition in the future. Job had this deep sense of destiny that his and Angie's future lay somewhere out west. He gritted his teeth and eased the poster back inside his shirt.

Having rode for two hours, Job pulled up to take a leak and let Red pull on some dry grass next to a wagon rut full of water. The weather had cleared some but the wind was still gusty and cold. Job was about to get back in the saddle when he heard singing. The sound was coming from around a bend in the road. He lifted the mules reins and walked on ahead to stretch his legs and see where the singing was coming from. There was the occasional pluck of what sounded like a banjo. North of the trail tucked up under a huge oak tree, Job saw the smoke from a campfire. Leaned against the tree was a feller in a top hat and a wool blanket over his lap. He was focused on the banjo and never saw Job walk up. There was a spring of water below the camp so Job led the mule in for a drink. The man was singing a tune to his own arrangement,

"Oh Suzanna, don't you cry for me, I'm off to Louisiana with my banjo on my knee. Oh Suzanna, Oh don't you fret for me, for if I can't find it in Louisiana, I'm off for Texas too!"

At the last chorus, the man looked up and nearly threw the banjo at Job. He never knew another soul was within ten miles. At first he just gazed at Job as he shifted the banjo to get to his feet.

Job decided to put him at ease and said, "Sounds pleasin' to me, don't get up for me," half grinning at the younger man. Immediately at Job's grin, the man's face lit up and he scrambled to his feet to approach Job.

"Howdy, Mister! Jimmy Bentley" he reached out to shake Job's hand. He never took his eyes off Job's pistol as he continued, "Coming outta B'ham and headin' out to Luzana and beyond. Obliged if you would jine me for a cup of coffee," he offered, pointing back at the campfire.

"Job Irvin." Job released his hand and replied in kind.

"I could use a break, been traveling since daybreak," he offered but not overly anxious to reveal his past and plans for the road ahead. Pop had told him he had two ears and one mouth, so listen twice as much as he spoke. Job hitched the mule close by the camp and brought out his tin cup. The man poured him a big swaller and retired to his pallet. Job kept standing, glad to be on his feet for a while. The coffee was excellent and he told Jimmy the same.

Job looked the camp over and noticed a nag of a horse tied in a thicket behind the oak. The camp was meager and there were no vittles in sight. Job took the conversation again, "Pretty good pickin' I heard, you a minstrel?" He asked.

"Awh, I play a few hoe downs and weddings but just for meals and to meet the gals," he answered.

"Don't let me stop yer playin'," Job offered for an opportunity to hear more.

"Got to pack it up and shoot me a rabbit or something 'fore dark," the boy said as he wrapped the banjo in a tote sack.

"You welcomed to stretch out here tonight, Mister," Jimmy went on rising from the ground.

"You short on grub?" Job was blunt and to the point and this caught Jimmy off guard. He hem hawed around kicking the dirt searching for what to say. "Got coffee and a couple of biscuits," he responded half heartedly.

"Tell you what," Job injected, "You play me a tune on that banjer and I'll pitch in the vittles," he offered.

"That's a deal!" Jimmy jumped at the offer.

The two men kicked around gathering the firewood then Job tended to his mule. He broke out the gunny sack Mrs. Cooper had packed with biscuits, salt pork and jar of wild honey. Jimmy's eyes lit up at the wild honey and salt pork. Job laid the grub out beside the fire and told Jimmy to hep himself while he rinsed off at the spring. The boy did just that and Job wondered how long the feller had gone without food. Freshened up a bit, he joined Jimmy at the fire. He spitted a piece of the pork over the fire just to be on the safe side. Salt pork sometimes gets a little tainted and Job was in no mood for the back door trots all night. The boy was good at brewing coffee and they settled in for the night with leisurely conversation.

"Livin' on the dangerous side travelin' alone, ain't ye?" Job asked.

"Nah! I know these trails as far as Meridian," Jimmy said.

"Any further, now, they tell me I'd better sleep with one eye open," he said chuckling.

"Headin' anyplace in particular?" Job queried.

"Maybe Jackson or New Orleans, I heered a minstrel could make a living pickin' and sanging down in the big town," he said hopefully.

"We might ride together, far as Jackson, you see fit," Job offered as Jimmy unwrapped the banjo and began to pluck away.

"That suits me just fine!" Jimmy remarked, and started into an old jingle,

"Fly in the buttermilk, shoo fly shoo. Fly in the buttermilk, shoo fly shoo. Fly in the buttermilk, shoo fly shoo. Shoo fly shoo my darling!"

Job grinned as he enjoyed the light hearted tune as he fixed his pallet to retire for the night. It was gonna be a cold one so he put on a couple of big chunks of oak wood for good measure. A whippoorwill began his chant in the thicket and Job reminisced the warm kiss he had enjoyed only hours before. He pulled the pistol to his arm pit as he fell into a good sleep.

CHAPTER 12

MERIDIAN, MISSISSIPPI

There was ice in the air the next morning as Job scrambled to fuel the long gone out fire. He made the coffee and had to rouse Jimmy from slumber. Job had never heard such snoring and mumbling from a sleeping person. He couldn't be resting carrying on in such a fashion, thought Job. He spitted the remainder of the salt pork and biscuits then took his breakfast, leaving some for Jimmy.

Job kind of took the lead, noticing the banjo person was not a morning person and saddled up and packed his mule while Jimmy ate breakfast. The boy finished up, led a sway back old mare out of the thicket and bridled her but with no saddle. Everything he owned must be in that tote sack he slung over his back, thought Job. There was no weapon of any kind to be seen on the feller.

For the next three days the two men rode from daylight to middle afternoon, or as much as the sway back could stand. Job kept a keen eye for game and they ate well on roasted game and crackers. The jar of wild honey sure helped out the bland diet. The morning of the fourth day they noticed farm shacks more often and Jimmy said Meridian was within shouting distance. Sure enough, within thirty minutes, Job could see a pall of smoke in the distance. They went from quiet countryside to hustle and bustle in minutes.

Job knew they needed to resupply with grub and he wanted to post a letter to Angie right away. He breached the matter with Jimmy who was all eyeballs and perked up at being in town.

71

"I got to find a dry goods store and post office, Jimmy," Job let him know as they rode into the busy town.

"Sure nuf, Job, I know just the place up ahead. It's a all in one and a man can get a shot of B-die and a gal too if'n he please," he cast an encouraging grin at Job.

Job had shared only limited information concerning the past six weeks. He knew the boy was very naïve and maybe just plain dumb about who he was riding along beside. Job simply stated, "Grub stake and post script a letter, don't do no rot gut," he said flatly.

Jimmy avoided eye contact and just nodded in consent. Not far ahead, he pointed to a large wood frame store front with a half dozen patron services printed across the front.

"Whatever you need, they got it!" he declared.

They rode up front to the hitching rail and dismounted, half hitching the animals to a post.

Jimmy hesitated and spoke to Job apologetically, "I kinda earn my keep as I go, Job. If I don't play, I don't eat," he said.

"You do what you gotta do but I won't tarry long," Job insisted, moving on inside the store.

The morning was too cold for stragglers outside. The pot bellied stove inside the store was surrounded by eight to ten locals, chewing and spitting in an old bucket.

It got as quiet as a morning after a Jack frost as they walked into the room. No one caught Job's eye but he could feel the searching eyes of the men.

Job moved on to the tables and shelves to gather the supplies as Jimmy stopped at the heater.

"Jimmy boy! Thought that was you!" the storekeep retorted.

"You bring that racket box?" he asked.

"Yes sir, rat here," Jimmy beamed unslinging the tote sack and breaking out the banjo.

"I got me a couple new melodies if you folks feelin' charitable." Jimmy propositioned, emphasizing charitable.

"Yeh! Play us one, I think I can spare a couple of ribs and a swaller of B-die," the old storekeep offered. All this time, Job noticed that he never took his eyes off of him.

Jimmy tuned up and broke into a hillbilly tune while the men admired his agile plucking of the banjo. It brought a much needed mood change into the room.

Job made several trips down the shelves, now that he was shopping for two mouths to feed. When he finished shopping, he settled at the register to post the letter and pay up. The storekeep tallied everything and took the letter Job offered.

Reading the address, the clerk retorted, "Johnson depot? Good feller. Mail rider came through yesterday with a big story about some Cherokee rescuing a white gal and pickin' up a huge reward." He studied Job's face for clues to his whereabouts.

"News to me," Job said, and counted out the receipt money.

He stacked his purchases in one arm keeping his pistol hand clear and headed for the door. Walking past Jimmy still strumming and plucking the banjo, he leaned down and whispered in his ear, "I'll be out west on the trail if you can catch up!" and he passed out the door.

Quickly Job packed away the grub and made his way out of town, knowing the storekeep had figured out who he was. Any thief in town would be looking for clues to his whereabouts. He had half way enjoyed Jimmy's company but if he couldn't keep up and do without his B-die, he would leave him.

Keeping his eyes peeled and pistol ready, Job never let up for two hours. Finally he came upon a good place where he could watch the trail and rest for a while. He gave the mule his due of corn and let him pull on a little grass. He leisurely carved out a chew of tobacco and watched the trail for Jimmy. Thirty minutes later, he gave up and took up the trail again.

Job was becoming a little concerned about the trail ahead. It was now the last week of February, tater planting time, and he needed information on the best route to Texas. The best he could figure was that he was still four or five weeks from the Sabine River crossing into Texas. Stories were told of white slavers or kidnappers shanghaiing lone travelers and enslaving them in the cotton fields of Mississippi and Louisiana. He was traveling alone and about half way lost. He would have to risk a stop for information on the trail west in the next few days. He sure would like to be on the Sabine River in the spring for rumor was there were jobs on the log floats and steamboats.

Job suddenly realized the jeopardy Jimmy had put him in staying behind like he did. The clerk and locals would pick the boy for information on Job and no telling how many were cold trailing him now. Job mounted Red and lit a shuck down the cold forbidden trail, glancing back occasionally for pursuers. Rumor had already swelled the reward to a fortune and this alone would draw flies.

Not running scared but feeling the urgency, Job pushed on into the cold night. He would ride the mule for a mile and walk for a quarter of a mile. Close to midnight, Job decided to bed down and do without a fire to be safe. For the next several days he would camp in the dark and enjoy his fire in the daylight. He would tie the mule down and bed down just out of stomping distance. Red would let him know if a strange man or animal was close by. Everything went well for the next two nights so Job relaxed his vigil and began to choose his camping sites to provide more comfort including a warm fire. He was getting lonely for conversation but never got past a wave or nod at travelers. One freight wagon nearly run him over as he halloed them for a word in passing. He had been told to be careful and people's reception so far past Meridian was skeptical and fearful.

CHAPTER 13

PEARL RIVER AND NEW FRIENDS

The change was subtle but the days were longer and Job noticed Jack Frost failed to visit a night or two. He didn't know exactly what to expect weather wise this far west of Georgia but it was a lot like home. You couldn't put your finger on it yet but there was a sheen of life peeping through the vegetation and especially evident on the open field. Job noticed small patches of rabbit grass along the open trail wherever sunlight lingered a couple of hours a day. As always, early spring made everyone feel better and everything looked better. Job was encouraged and relieved to be on the move again, alone.

Job had noticed a crude map tacked to the wall of the store back in Meridian. It showed Jackson, Mississippi some hundred miles due west. He had put a good fifty miles behind and noticed pig trails leading off the big road to small farms more frequent everyday. He was hoping to chance upon a hospitable conversation and glean some traveling news.

Having stopped to water and graze the mule, Job suddenly got all the company and attention a man could want in one day. He had mixed emotions about what he saw approaching but hoped they had answers he needed about the trail ahead.

A company of U.S. Calvary troopers were headed his way taking up the trail for a quarter of a mile. Job walked the mule a little further off the road and waited the passersby's. There was what looked like a Captain followed by a Lieutenant and Master Sergeant out front. The Lieutenant had pointed at Job and had said something to the Captain. The troop was called to a halt and all eyes were on Job. His chest tightened a bit for he was reminded of the horror stories Pop had told of the inhumane treatment of Indians and non-whites by Federal troops. Prejudice and bias was ingrained in the military so Job needed to be careful for the next little while.

The Captain spoke first, "Mornin' Mister! Identification and destination may I ask." He very businesslike prompted Job, not giving even the courtesy of eye contact. The Master Sergeant was scrutinizing Job and had a silly half grin on his face. Job could tell they were used to having their way and would give them no chance to exert their authority.

"Yes sir! Job Irvin. Outta Atlanta, Georgia and headin' out to Texas for possibilities. My paper is in the saddle bag if you would allow me." Job gestured at the mule and the officer nodded to fetch the paper. Job pulled the family Bible out carefully unwrapping it and pulled the birth certificate out to hand to the officer.

A second scowl crossed the face of the old Sergeant and he popped off instinctively, "A religious Injun?" There was a ripple of grunts back down the ranks till the Captain cut his eyes at the Sergeant. Immediately a quiet pall fell back over the troopers.

The Captain surveyed the document and handed it gingerly back to Job. "Cherokee?" the Captain asked calmly.

"Yes sir, mother's side." Job replied. There was a snicker from the Sergeant.

The officer continued, "Guard that document with your life! If you lose it, head north of the Red River and stay there!"

Job had no idea what he was hearing and replied as much, "What's going on out there?" Job inquired.

"All Injun clans along the Sabine River are given land north of the Red River to relocate and settle. Only U.S. citizens can own land and slaves in Texas," he stated emphatically.

Job felt a deep disgust at what was being said and knew the same politics were already working out west that had swept through Georgia a generation ago. He listened and nodded in agreement and ventured to garner a little information on the trail ahead.

"Sir, how far is it to Jackson and where's the best crossing into Texas?" he asked politely.

The officer had relaxed a bit in the saddle and seemed to enjoy a little conversation from a civilian.

"Half days ride out to Jackson. East side of town pick up the Natchez trail headin' southeast and cross the Ol' Miss at Natchez. They's a Coushatta trail bearing southwest out of Alexandria, Luzana and the old El Camino Real due west into Nacogdoches, Texas. I'd take up the Kings Highway and work south down the Sabine. Hang on to that paper and sleep with one eye open!" the officer advised as he reined his horse back into the trail, lifted his hand and the Lieutenant gave movement commands. The old Sergeant didn't like what he heard and saw and let Job know it in a scowl as he rode away.

Job watched the last troopers disappear down the trail and replaced the document and Bible. He wrote down the names of the towns and trails that the officer gave him. He knew the Spanish and Mexicans had scoured Texas and parts of Louisiana for a couple hundred years and was anxious to see this foreign land. He was surprised at the clear warning by the Army officer and decided to be extra cautious from this day forward. Encouraged by how close he was to Jackson, Mississippi he mounted Red and turned down the trail into the sunset.

The trail wided into a maze of potholes and hog wallows full of mire as Job got closer to Jackson. The big wheel single axle wood carts only beat out more holes avoiding one another. Job was hoping to camp close to water to freshen up and get a note written to Pop and Angie before dark. A while later he got his wish for water but he didn't know what he would do with what occupied both banks of the Pearl River. Both sides of the river had become one huge campground of every sort of traveler. There were mule pens next to the water, dozens of freight wagons and wood carts and what looked like a wagon train of west bound settlers making camp. Reining in the mule, he dismounted and observed the melee for a while deciding what to do next. He settled on a campsite between the wagon train of settlers and the river. The mule teams were down stream and maybe the water could be used without a settling bucket. He walked Red to a lone holly bush and went about making camp.

There was plenty going on during the late evening hour before dark. Mule skinners were cussing their animals and children running off energy close to the wagon train. From their tack and wagon quality Job figured these folks were out of Georgia or the Carolinas. They were an organized bunch and there was nothing frivolous or unnecessary hanging on their wagons. He wondered if they might be headed to Texas or the Oregon territory.

Job removed the saddle and bags from Red and tied one corner of the tarp to the holly bush. There wasn't a sprig of firewood within a mile of the camp so Job approached a wood hauler set up for that reason. The old man offered him all he could carry in two trips for two bits. Two arm loads would be plenty for supper and breakfast but Job had learned a few tricks on doing chores growing up. He squatted like a Chinaman sorting rice and stacked wood higher than his head, then pushed up with both legs. He could hear the old gent mumble a few choice expletives as he walked away with the second arm load. A couple of men from the wagon train had approached to buy wood and they were grinning at Job's antics.

A big blond headed fellow commented as Job walked past, "Maybe we could hire you to make our trade for kindlin'?" he chuckled. Everyone laughed except the old wood hauler.

Job got his fire going and took the coffee can and Red up the riverbank in sight of camp to drink and fetch water. A huge trestle bridge crossed the river and things were a mess on both sides and underneath the span. What Job hadn't noticed till now was a chain gang of eight African slaves beneath the trestle. They were passing a bucket between one another rinsing off and drinking the nasty water. An armed overseer stood leisurely by daydreaming. These were some tough people, thought Job. All the men were barefoot and scantly dressed and the water must be fifty degrees cold.

Disgusted at the spectacle, Job fetched the water and led the mule back to his camp. Shortly he had his coffee and was gnawing on a cracker watching the evening hustle and bustle at the bridge. The men at the wagon train were hob nobbin' as their womenfolk tended to their cook fires. Job decided to see what he could learn on their destination. He took his coffee tin along and strolled up to the men gathered at their fire.

The yeller haired fellow grinned as Job walked up and remarked, "I hope he's not after firewood!" and the others laughed.

Job took the cue and extended a hand to greet the strangers. "Job, Atlanta, Georgia," he offered.

"You don't say? Big Miller and Spike, from the Carolinas," they both shook Job's hand rigorously.

"Don't want to sound nosy but I'm headin' for Texas and thought maybe you folks were likeminded." Job offered.

"Oregon territory," the big fellow replied.

Spikes, the smaller and quieter man spoke up, "Well, most folks headed nor' west into Missouri to pick up the trail. We heard so much about opportunity in Texas, we decided to give it a look see."

"We decided to move on. We hope to trek south of the Red River and Indian country and find our way into Bent's Fort, Kansas." Miller, the big man added.

The men talked on till dark and Job was invited to a bowl of tater soup. He offered a little history concerning his raising and family. He never mentioned his heritage.

Big Miller made an offer that was mighty appealing to Job. "Job, if you not in too big a hurry, you welcomed to jine our party. They tell me bigger is better up ahead and I believe you are an honorable feller." Miller was to the point and honest.

Job blushed a little and said, "Preciate that. I've fretted over what to do next for a week. I don't think I could hook up with a better lot than what I see in you folks. I'm with you!" Job grinned, reaching out to accept the offer with a handshake. Everyone seemed relieved and Big Miller announced the news to the family making ready for bed. The train made up a Conestoga and a freight wagon full of plows and dry goods. Job counted six children around the fire and two women.

Big Miller invited Job to move in under a wagon if he pleased and he was more that glad. He eased off to his camp with two toe headed boys wanting to help. Big Miller and Spike looked at one another in a self satisfied way. Without saying a word they both knew what the other was thinking. Here was a decent, hard working man that was as comfortable with a hog leg in his belt and a pig sticker tucked in his boot as they were with a plow in their hand. You couldn't put a price on this asset where they were headed. They both thanked God for such good fortune.

CHAPTER 14

TRAIL BOSS

Job and his new friends were breaking camp and harnessing the mules at daybreak while the ladies fried corn fritters and served them with molasses and hot coffee. Job felt an eagerness and sense of absolute purpose just being around honest, hard working people like these. They had their ways and routines and Job just helped out when they let him. The children all had chores and there was a light hearted kindness that mellowed the difficult pioneer burden they were under. He noticed someone read from the Good Book before bedtime and after meals. He caught himself daydreaming that Angie would walk from behind a wagon any moment. Everyone was ready and in their places watching the river crossing melee.

Big Miller and Spike approached Job and Miller said, "Job, we not insinuating one thang, but you seem to know your way in worldly things and such. We'd like you to be our trail boss or spokesman if the need arises." Job could see the sincerity and dependency of the men asking for guidance and was deeply humbled.

"Yeah, I seen a few things and been in a few scrapes if that matters. If we run into trouble up ahead, I just ask that you trust my judgment and see our decisions through. These women and children are gonna be weighed in the balance in everything I do."

"Amen, brother! So be it." Spike spoke up enthusiastically.

With that settled, Job rode out ahead and waited for Big Miller's signal from the lead wagon and he led off on crossing the bridge. Traffic alternated from one side to another. When Job's time came, he raised his arm to the other side waving two fingers, indicating his two wagon train. He couldn't help but feel a little pride in passing over ahead of such a clean outfit. Ten minutes later they were all clear of the crossing and trekking through a multitude of every sort. Jackson was a major crossroads and chaos was the only word to describe the movement of commerce. After two hours of dodging ruts and reckless freight wagons, the wagon train broke out on the west side of town and could breathe a little deeper. Everything was dusted over with a red colored sheen, mostly dried animal manure ground to powder beneath the thousands of hooves and wagon wheels daily. Job waved the wagons over next to a smitty and dry goods store for a break. Everyone piled out and beat and brushed the dust and stink from one another. The mules were blowin' and snortin' their displeasure of the past few miles.

The ladies tended to the wagons while the men visited the hardware store and then they would get their turn to purchase essentials. Job had added a few lines to his note to Missy about his good fortune in joining the wagon train. He also posted a letter to Pop in Savannah and another to Tom Hall and his family. His purchases included fifty extra rounds of .44 ammo, two plugs of tobacco, two pounds of grain for the mule, a pound of coffee and a pack of salt and pepper. Noticing the candy jars, Job grabbed a handful of horehound and rock candy for the children and his mule. Red expected a sweet treat anytime they visited a store and would show his displeasure if not satisfied. He loved tobacco more than Job but that was a little too expensive habit. Job had tried to substitute coffee grounds and chicory but Red didn't buy it.

In conversation with the storekeep, the men learned they were less than two miles from the Natchez Trace that ran southwest from Jackson to Natchez, Mississippi and the ferries there. An old survey map on the wall showed at least a hundred twenty miles to Natchez with an Army post about halfway between the cities. The storekeep followed the men to the porch and commented on the mule teams.

"You better sleep with yo' mules in that country. They prized moren' a woman on the Missip'." He grinned and went back inside.

The men took over the wagons while the ladies did their purchasing. Job pitched in a dollar for spuds anticipating a dutch oven full of smothered taters and onions. The children couldn't have been more pleased in their new found friend. Job broke out the candy and the kids went wild. Red went to working his ears and eyeballin' Job for his piece of candy.

An hour later the little wagon train was on the trace headed southwest outta Jackson. Job couldn't believe the wagon ruts and mud holes to navigate. He had figured two weeks travel to Natchez but unless the trail cleared a little, it would take a week longer. The storekeep informed them of a place called White Oak camp, ten miles out and the men decided to push for it before dark. Running water was essential health wise and every decision or stop was based upon the water source.

As they traversed the rough wagon road, Job mentioned something the storekeep had said about the mules. "Probably time we set up night watch if I heard the clerk right back there." Job offered more as seeking advice than an order.

"That's on my mind too," Big Miller agreed.

"Ya'll think about it but I'd like to take the graveyard watch seeing ya'll have family to take care of." Job offered wanting to keep harmony in the families.

The men talked on and shared other concerns they might face down the trail. Job had never seen a weapon among these folks and finally asked what they were packing. Both men had purchased a new Colt Dragon for the trek west but were not familiar with the art of weaponry. They agreed on a crash course in gun handlin' soon as possible. Job had never killed a man and he told them what his daddy had said on the matter. Hate and discrimination of the Indian had made it necessary to take up arms in defense. Tad Irvin had told Job never to draw his pistol unless absolutely necessary and that you could stop a man without killing him. The Cherokee considered all men's lives as sacred but would not flinch to protect their family from an enemy. Job expressed his daddy's philosophy on self defense but never revealed his Indian heritage.

Job was surprised at what Spike said next. "They ain't but two kinda people that believe it like that, and that's a Bible believing man or an Injun," he said honestly. Both Spike and Big Miller seemed to leave the door open for honesty. There was a twinkle of mirth in their eyes and Job thought it best to get it over with and let the chips fall where they may.

"Mother was Cherokee." He offered unapologetically but civilly.

Big Miller guffawed out loud like he had waited for this moment.

"We know'd it! Matter of fact, everybody at the Jackson crossing could see it when you rode up to the river!" Spike was chuckling about it now.

"There are some greedy land grabbers that was behind the Trail 'o Tears that connived and lied till half the poor whites in Carolina ended up share croppers!" Big Miller chipped in understandingly.

"Jesus Christ was a man of color, so what's all the fussin' about?" Spike tossed the question out honestly seeking clarity on the issue that was a hot bed across the south lately.

"It's filthy lucre, money! they usin' civil rights, states rights and sovereignty crap to cover for greed. The love of money is the root of all evil!" Big Miller gave a brief sermon in answer to Spike's inquiry.

"Yeah, it's a mess, them politics. Anyway, I 'preciate you folks layin' yore cards out with me. But I got to warn you. I could be a thorn in your side down the road. Lot of folks prejudice towards Indians and color out there." Job wanted to give fair warning suspecting these folks were a little naïve about racism.

"Don't fret none Job, you're kinfolks as far as I am concerned. Man touch you, he jest touched my family. I swear to God by that!" Big Miller's voice rose emotionally. Job then knew he had a back to back friend for life.

"Same here, Job, you can count on me. I'll be there for you," Spike agreed, tipping his sweat stained hat at Job.

They all rode on in silence but some ingredient had been added to this group of west bound settlers, an alloy of brotherhood and commitment toward one another. A feller trespass these folks and he would bite off more than he could chew! Job felt a peace and contentment he had not known since before his parents died.

CHAPTER 15

HOLSTERS FOR PISTOLS

Mules are the best at picking out the safest and easiest route and the wagons made good time into White Oak. A fast running creek crossed the trail beneath an eighty foot tall white oak tree. Two or three acres had been worn down by past travelers on both sides of the creek. A log bridge spanned the creek which had been chinked with mud and tree limbs over the years till a solid span emerged. The area was clean as a whistle as folks had used up every sprig of firewood for a hundred yards.

Not knowing how crowded the camp could be before dark, Job decided to make the creek crossing before stopping to camp. It was early evening and the only other folks in sight were the same party of overseers and slaves they had seen in Jackson. They had made the crossing also and pulled up next to the water. Two white men were transporting the eight black men in the freight wagon pulled by two mules. They had been seated on the ground and chained to a tree. They were chewing on what looked like parched corn and lard tack. An old dipper gourd served to quench their thirst. This spectacle would make the campsite bitter sweet but they had no alternative. Job's party pulled up across the road from the slavers.

Less than an hour later camp was made and coffee served. The leftover firewood from the Jackson crossing came in handy for starters. The ladies had learned of Job's crave for smothered taters and onions and set about fixin' supper. The children were gathering firewood while the men tended the mules and harness.

Job's thoughts were on the trail ahead and the dangers lurking there. The wild animals could be dealt with but the two legged kind were unpredictable and merciless. He had been handed the burden of safe passage for these folks and he was preparing for the worst. He had seen a roll of cured cowhide tied to the freight wagon and asked Bill Miller its purpose.

"Tie down straps and such. What you got in mind?" he asked.

"I seen a pistol holster on a feller in Jackson that looked mighty handy. I"d like a piece to try and fashion one for my shooter." Job explained.

"Hep yourself, they's a punch and anvil in there if you need it." Miller offered.

Job broke the leather out and cut a piece big enough for what he needed. This was fine cured leather and he didn't want to waste an inch. He folded the leather around his pistol a half a dozen times till he was satisfied with the feel then took his skinning knife to make the cut. He had been taught the art of leatherwork and weaving by his Cherokee mother and went about the task swiftly and expertly. The children had gathered around to watch him cut, tuck, punch holes and cut strips for binding. The ladies nodded their approval at one another watching his dexterity with the knife and stitching.

An hour later Job had himself a pattern and he tried it on for fit. There was a shoulder strap, waist band and tube attached with a leg strap at the end. The style would have the holster riding at a forty five degree angle just above the waist with the pistol grip just above the navel. After several frustrating adjustments, he was pleased enough to punch the eyes and begin the stitching.

Job had hastened the holster chore for a reason. He wanted to display their fire power to any adversary or thief they may encounter.

"An ounce of prevention is worth a pound of cure." Pop always said.

If he could get this rig serviceable, he would fashion a holster for the other two men. They would have to get used to wearing the harness in public. He knew it wouldn't go over well with the farmers but they would have to comply. A thief or robber would think twice before crossing tracks with three men packing iron in this fashion.

The ladies had timed taking supper before dark and the smell of potatoes and onions filled the campsite. The slaves were gazing at the dutch oven advertising the delectable inside. The slaves never took their eyes from the ground but Job knew that they must be tortured by the smell of cooked food. Big Miller had already made acquaintance with the overseers and he crossed the road again. There was a discussion and Job noticed Big Miller pointing at the slaves while talking. He hoped the man did not stir any trouble over the slaves.

The ladies called for supper and everyone washed up at the creek. The children got in line like little soldiers at the serving pot and so Job joined the game and stepped in line.

"That's all we need, is another kid to feed!" a mother remarked and they all laughed at Job.

Everyone found a place to sit and Spike said the grace.

As everyone ate, Big Miller spoke, "I just spoke with the slavers over yonder and invited to feed 'em if we could feed the Aferkans too." They hem hawed around about it but agreed finally. When we eat all we want, I'd like to feed those poor folks." He glanced at Job as he finished talking.

Everyone was nodding in agreement and Job said, "That's the right thing to do Big, and I'll help anyway I can."

No one went for second helpings and the ladies had pulled out an old newsprint and tore it into ten squares. They divided the potatoes on the make do plates with a piece of cornbread. As Job watched, the two families gathered up the vittles and marched over to the slave camp. The two white overseers removed their hats as the ladies approached and shouted "Heah!" at the slaves. The black men all stood at once and an overseer gestured for the ladies to hand the food to the slaves. The men had no idea how to respond. One overseer took one fellers hand and laid the dab of potatoes on his palm and gestured to eat. They went down the line till all had food and the overseer yelled again, "Heah!" and they all sat back down. The overseers carried on with the ladies about how delicious the food was. The children stood moon eyed and silent while watching the black captives eat. Job thought what a good example these parents were setting for their kids. He absolutely detested the notion of slavery but at least they had attempted to relieve their suffering.

The slavers carried on about not being able to repay their kindness and Big Miller told them what Job had said, "Just pass it on!"

Around the campfire that evening, Job showed off his new fangled holster and put forth the idea for the men to start packing their weapons daily. The ladies looked a little concerned but all agreed they would rather be ready for trouble or maybe discourage others from making trouble. Job started the men fashioning their holsters and the ladies pitched in their expertise. In two hours all three men were wearing finished holsters stuffed with a hog leg pistol. Job decided on a three hour watch for the men and he would always take the midnight to three watch. This would make it easier on the family men and he figured if anything went down, it would happen after midnight.

Pop had always told him, "Snakes crawl at night and specially when its quiet!"

The wind had picked up blowing before midnight and thunder could be heard off to the north and the flash of lightening was more often now. Everyone shuffled around in the dark buttoning everything down as water tight as possible. Sure enough, within the hour, a cold norther moaned and whined as it pushed its way through the tall timber. The temperature dropped thirty degrees in minutes and Job positioned himself behind a pin oak for a windbreak as he began his watch for the night. It looked like a dry norther and Job was glad of that. A toad strangler rain could make the trace impossible for the heavy wagons. There were bog holes and wagon ruts two feet deep along the trail where travelers had been stranded. It could take three or four days for a dirt road to dry enough to pass over with heavy wagons.

It looked like they were going to luck out on this storm and Jobs thoughts turned to Angie and what she was doing and thinking on this cold night. He loved and missed his own family that he had lost to disease but nothing had prepared him for the loneliness he felt and the longing he had to hold that woman to his bosom again. His daddy had said at marriage he would become as one flesh with his wife. Job felt like Angie was already a part of him. She strolled gracefully through his mind and burned deep in his heart. Often he was startled because he thought he caught the scent of her sweetness. Not too far down the road, he would do whatever was necessary to see her again, he thought. The wind continued to howl and the temperature to drop as Job snuggled in the warmth of his tarp and thoughts of Angie.

CHAPTER 16

LOVE STORY

The dry norther roared across the open potato field of the Cooper farm and scattered every loose object and rattled every latch on the place. Angie Cooper was awakened and lay listening to the cold wind whispering and at times howling in gusts at the resisiting tree tops. She was hoping this would be the last cold spell before Spring. Her mother had contracted a bad cough and maybe the warmer spring air and getting outside would help her.

Being shut in by the weather was too hard as she tried to sort out her feelings about Job. She hated being cooped up and wanted to be busy doing something to pass the time. The chores were caught up, thanks to Job, and now they could only wait for spring planting. She had read every book in the house at least three times. The Bible was required reading after supper and she enjoyed that.

It had been two weeks since Job had rode away and she seemed to miss him more each day. She had moped around for days now and her mother could see that she was love sick and would only get worse till a letter from Job arrived. A letter from out west could take months but Ellen dared not tell her daughter that fact. She decided to spend some time in heart to heart conversation with Angie and share her love story with her. No one but her parents and Ely knew the whirlwind romance they had enjoyed. She by no means wanted to push her daughter into an overnight fling but she knew the girl needed encouragement and confidence. She could imagine Angie's dreams and hopes for she had endured the same heartache and thrills. It was time to let her daughter know that love would find a way in her life.

One morning after breakfast, Ellen found the opportunity to sit down in confidence with her daughter. Ely was at the potato shed mending harnesses and would be there till dinner. The dishes and kitchen were cleaned so Ellen took the opportunity before Angie followed her daddy outside.

"Angie, would you like to hear how I met Ely and the romance that followed?" She sat in her favorite chair and smiling at Angie she pointed to an easy chair in front of her.

Angie hesitated a moment, her eyes big and mouth gaped open in surprise. "A romance? Mother! You're kiddin'! You and daddy romancin'?"

Ellen was surprised at how incredulous she had sounded to her daughter but realized this subject had never crossed her threshold before.

"That's what I said, silly! Now sit down and let me tell you a real live love story!" she giggled in anticipation of what she would reveal to her precious daughter.

"Yes, mam, and I want to hear every tidbit, you hear mother? I'm grown now and don't be too modest." Angie insisted as she settled into her chair for the duration of her mother's story.

Ellen got situated and began her tale. "I didn't always live out here on the farm. I was born and raised a city girl. My daddy, Bob Sanders and mother, Nell, owned and operated a dry goods store in B'ham. I was prim and proper and educated.

I had my coming out party when I was sixteen and a dozen suitors attended!"

Angie butted in immediately, "What is a coming out party, mother?"

It hurt Ellen to explain because Angie never had such a wonderful event here in the country. The closest neighbor here was three miles away and only one child, a girl.

"Honey, in town when a girl turns sixteen, her parents hold a social event and invites all the local eligible boys to visit for a party. There was cake and punch, fidlin', dancing and everyone dressed in their Sunday best."

"My Lord, what have I missed in life?" Angie lamented, but got on a lighter side quickly. "Okay, mother, go ahead. I'll try to wait till you finish before I ask another question." She pressed for the story to continue.

Ellen knew her daughter better than that but was already having fun and continued, "I had several serious suitors. I was having the time of my

89

life playing the field, mind you. There were boys I had crushes on and puppy love set in at times. Now all of this was under the hawk eyes of mother and daddy. Daddy culled the boys out until only two or three had the nerve to ask him to come calling. Daddy and mother never tolerated no lazy boy or one with a bad character to hang around. I'm so glad now that they towed the line for me." Ellen had closed her eyes and laid her head back reminiscing her good parents. She came back to the moment before Angie could say anything and continued again.

"I was so full of myself and manipulative of others that I was swept completely off my feet emotionally when your daddy walked into the store. He and his daddy had walked in to pick up a few things for the farm. I noticed how handsome Ely was but Lordy was he bashful! I could tell he was eyeballin' me and finally caught him with a smile. Honey, he turned red as a ripe tomato!" Ellen stated grinning.

"Mom! You were that bold with strange boys?" Angie blurted out.

"Not every boy, Angie, mainly Ely. He was so different than the town boys. He was simple and quiet but Lord he moved with the confidence of a panther! I was afraid they would leave and I would never know his name. I will never forget how my opportunity came to meet him up close."

"Mr. Cooper told Ely to get fitted for a work shirt and he approached me to ask for help but could only mumble and point to the material shelf. I was very curt and gave him his options, Cotton or wool, grey or plain. He choose the grey cotton and I choose one to lay against his shoulders for fit. All was well till I laid my hands against his shoulders and looked up into those green eyes of his. Honey, time stood still and my knees grew weak as water. We both were embarrassed but liked what we felt."

Angie couldn't stand the suspense and asked, "Did you kiss him?"

"Heavens no! I had just met the man. It was like all my dreams of the love of my life stood before me." Ellen crossed her arms to her bosom emphasizing how dear the moment was to her.

"You mean ya'll never said nothin'?" Angie asked.

"Yes, Ely told me his name and where he lived and I told him my name and that he was in my daddy's store. We rattled on a while and I got his shirt tied up. I slipped a note in the shirt pocket asking him to come back and visit. They finished their business in town and returned home." Ellen finished.

Ellen rose and walked to the kitchen window to watch the cold wind sway the tall timbers in the distance. She could see Ely going about his chores. She knew Angie was in love and was in for a long wait before she saw Job again. She wanted to choose her words well and prepare her for the struggles that lay ahead. She took a glass of water and returned to her chair. The mild cough had grown persistent and she wanted to finish her story.

"Did daddy come callin'?" Angie asked.

"No. There was a long waiting period, Angie. Five weeks went by and I never saw or heard from Ely. Mother had noticed me moping around and got me to confide in her. I told her about Ely and she said it was probably puppy love and it would pass. She never scolded me or took me lightly. She did carry on how nice and mannered Ely was and I knew she was on my side. I told her I thought of Ely all the time and that I had even dreamed of him!"

Angie broke in not able to contain her feeling and revelations of what she was hearing.

"Mother! I dream of Job! We talk and its so real to me. Sometimes I can even smell him mother!" Tears had filled Angie's eyes and began to course down her cheeks. She sniffed and dried her eyes on her blouse sleeve.

"I guess I sound plumb silly." Angie defended her emotions.

Ellen was quick to encourage her daughter. These were feelings that would sustain her and she needed to know that.

"No! No! Honey! These are good things. They are feelings of genuine love and concern. You are bonding to Job and you must cherish these feelings. True love must not be taken for granted! Now, let me finish my story. We're getting to the good part now!" Ellen deliberately perked up to fortify Angie's honesty. Taking a deep breath she continued.

"Weeks had gone by and suddenly one day, there he was. He and his father were in town to see the blacksmith. I was sweeping the front porch as they passed and our eyes met briefly. He tipped his hat and smiled at me and my world stopped honey! I knew I was in love with that man." Ellen stated.

"Mother, that's the feelings I have for Job. Aside from the fact he was my rescuer and was so decent and protective of me. I love him on his own merits. Our spirits are knitted together and he feels the same for me." Angie finished, wanting her mother to continue.

"Let's see now," Ellen continued, "Ely and his daddy had brought in busted wheels to be repaired at the cooper shop and smitty. The job kept them in town overnight and that evening Ely came by the store. He was wearing the grey shirt I had fitted for him. He meddled around in the store till he got courage enough to speak to me. We shared pleasantries and finally he asked permission to approach daddy about calling on me Sunday afternoon. He also wanted me to meet his daddy."

Angie chuckled in dismay at her daddy's boldness and urgency. "You mean daddy moved in on you that fast?" she asked.

"Yes indeed! It was like a whirlwind and all the weeks gone by not seeing Ely only made it sweeter!" Ellen laughed with her daughter.

"I did not know at the time but I had an ally. Daddy! He played dumb and a little ornery but later told me he was delighted in the arrangement." Ellen's eyes misted over remembering her daddy.

Bob Sanders knew his daughter and kept tabs on the local boys and prospective suitors. He would never approve but a couple of the young men to see his daughter formally. She was playing the field and he had to be on guard constantly.

Ellen was fiercely independent and industrious and this virtue weeded out most callers. Bob had hoped and prayed for a man of character in his daughter's life and low and behold, she had one now!" Standing in front of him with his hat in his hand was the answer to Bob's prayer and he was not sure what to do with him.

Ely spoke to Bob, "Mr. Sanders, I am Ely Cooper and I live out of town a day's ride from here. I am Bo and Doris Cooper's son," he stated flatly.

Bob didn't want to sound too anxious or knowing of what was happening between the two young people and replied casually, "Sure son, I been knowin' your family close to twenty years now. What can I help you with?" He gazed around the room pretending to offer assistance with the merchandise.

"I don't need to buy anything, Mr. Sanders. I would like permission to escort Miss Ellen to the Cooper shop to meet my daddy. Also, Miss Ellen said it was okay to call on her Sunday afternoon if you permitted."

Ely had said it all in one breath and Bob thought the lad would faint before he finished speaking. Bob had never seen such a sincere and hopeful look in a young man's eyes and it humbled him. He didn't want to be careless or hasty in his response but he couldn't help but like this young farmer.

"Tell you what, you visit here with Ellen and let me talk to her mother first." He stated very businesslike and turned to find Mrs. Sanders at the rear of the store.

Nell Sanders was aware of everything going on in her daughters life and knew what was coming as Bob approached her sheepishly. She had noticed the change in her daughter's demeanor the day the Cooper lad visited the store over a month ago. Ellen had seemed to grow up overnight or maybe she had not accepted the fact her baby girl was now a young adult.

Ellen had entertained her suitors, had her crushes on a few boys and been sick with puppy love but nothing serious, until now. This strapping young lad from the wilderness had charmed her daughter. She was now very distant and curt with the other boys and even acted more responsible and ladylike.

Bob saw the knowing look on his wife's face and knew she had been listening to him and Ely. He didn't want to be hasty but he felt good about the young man waiting for an answer.

"Nell, I think we have a serious suitor on our hands. He's Bo and Doris Cooper's son and he passes muster as far as I'm concerned. You know Ellen better than I do, so you better speak to the boy." He offered his opinion gingerly. What she said next threw him for a loop.

"Bob, that young man is good for Ellen. I never seen a woman so affected by a man, 'cept in my case over you." She grinned and reached up to pinch his cheek. "She's in deep water now and all we can do is help her swim. Introduce me to this shining Prince." Nell laughed and followed Bob to the front of the store where Ely stood waiting.

"Ely, I'd like you to meet my wife, Nell."

Ely reached out and nervously shook her hand, replying, "Good day, Mam."

Nell spoke first, "Son, I understand you have asked to call on my daughter?"

"Yes Mam, if you please," Ely replied.

"Well, we think highly of your parents but don't really know you. But on the reputation of your parent's good name, I will give my consent for you to see my daughter on Sunday afternoons, in public of course." Nell finished her part with pursed lips and glanced at Bob for his reply.

The blood had returned to Ely's face and Bob wanted to get the suspense over for the lad. He couldn't conceal his pleasure from anyone.

"Ely, I agree with Nell. We will lay down some rules on visitation and expect you to comply. You can tell Ellen that you have our permission to call on her." Bob smiled and shook Ely's hand and he and Nell returned to work.

Ely walked to the front porch where Ellen pretended to be sweeping while waiting on an answer from her parents. His hat was in his hand and his eyes cast to the floor as he walked up. She did not know what to expect not being able to see his face.

Ely lifted his head and looked into her beautiful eyes and said, "Miss Ellen Sanders, I have requested consent and received the same from your parents to call on you every Sunday afternoon for the rest of my life!" He grinned as he spoke, watching her eyes fill with joy and tears.

Ellen never dreamed a farm boy could be so eloquent and decided to play along to keep from crying.

"Why, Ely Cooper, I think I may be able to find you a spot on my long list of suitors on Sunday afternoons." She broke out giggling and took his big brown hand in hers.

Ely continued, "I also have permission to escort you to the stables to meet my daddy if it would please you." He donned his hat and bowed at the waist with his right arm extended to receive hers. Ellen adjusted her bonnet and took his arm as they strolled down the street talking and laughing.

CHAPTER 17

LOVE WILL FIND A WAY

Bob and Nell Sanders watched from the front door till they were out of sight. Both had tears in their eyes but a great joy and peace had filled their hearts and minds. Some things you just know is meant to be and they both agreed they were witnessing such an event.

Bo Cooper saw the young couple coming down the street and he figured he knew what was brewing. Since their last trip to town over a month ago his son had been inquisitive and energetic as a buck deer in rut. Each day he would ask if anything was needed from town. He warted his daddy about where and when he had met mother and how long they had courted.

Doris Cooper cornered her husband one evening and asked if Ely had met a girl in town. Bo only remembered the girl at the store that had fit his shirt. To this she got a humorous look on her face and replied, "Your son is in love and you better put the fire out or else get him back to town before he goes nuts!" she laughed out loud.

"Oh, he's my son now?" Bo shot back.

"Yes, he needs to hear more about Adam and Eve instead of the birds and bees." She advised her husband.

Ely and Ellen were approaching the wagon where Bo was working and they grew quiet as he rose to greet them. He removed his hat to greet Ellen and spoke to Ely, "Son, I don't remember ordering a pretty lady from the store." He grinned at Ellen and both her and Ely turned blood red.

"Pa, I'd like you to meet Miss Ellen Sanders." Ely beamed introducing her to his Pa.

"Nice to meet you Mam." Bo responded nicely.

"Mister Cooper, good day." Ellen curtsied and Ely almost burst adoring her.

"Let's move to the shade for a cool drink of water." Bo offered kindly. He rinsed his face and hands and offered the couple to sit a minute. They sat on a slab bench and Ely lost no time getting to the point.

"Pa, "I been knowing Ellen for a while now and her parents, Mr. and Mrs. Sanders, just gave me permission to call on her Sunday afternoon . . . course if it's okay with you and mama!" He dumped it all on Bo at once and left him in an awkward position. He wouldn't dare embarrass his son in public so he picked his words carefully to reply.

"Mam, you come from a very respectful family that I have been friends with and been a patron of theirs for years. Why, I remember when you were born. Anyway, Ely is a grown man and if this is what you two want, I'll agree to it as long as he is respectful of your parent's wishes." He emphasized.

The faces of the young couple lit up with relief and Bo was glad it went well. He would advise his son later on these spur of the moment decisions and not warning him. They excused themselves to return to the store and Bo went back to work on the wagon.

Ellen had a coughing spell and paused to get a drink of water.

"When was his first visit and what happened? Did ya'll kiss?" Angie asked, giving her mother a knowing glance.

"Some things are personal and private, Honey. You'll have to fill in the blanks on that." She grinned slyly. "Ely came the following Sunday and it was heaven on earth! He stayed so late that he had to ride home in the dark!" she remembered so well now.

"After six visitations we realized we couldn't live without one another so Ely asked daddy for my hand in marriage." She recalled.

"Daddy and mama set up a get together for our families to meet one Sunday to make the wedding arrangements. These were some busy days and nights but we all had a barrel of fun. Mama made my dress and the Methodist preacher called our vows. We lived with Ely's parents until our cabin was built. It was a very difficult time but I would do it again."

Ellen had kept these wonderful events in her heart to share with her daughter and she wept with joy while telling them. With all the conviction she could muster, she finished by saying, "Angie, love will find a way! Keep yourself strong and be ready when Job calls, love will find a way!"

The story her mother told gave Angie more hope and purpose than ever now. She and her mother had this mutual joy between them now and it bewildered Ely. He just passed it off as a woman thing. He missed the young man Job but figured he was the reason his daughter was so unpredictable lately.

Ellen Cooper had not been well when Angie had been kidnapped and presumed dead. Tuberculosis and losing her only child had caused a nervous breakdown. Angie's return had been a miracle that gave her opportunity to share her feelings with her daughter. The toll of the past several months had been too much on her already diseased body. Two weeks after her heart to heart with Angie, she developed pneumonia and died a couple of days later.

Ely sent word by a mail carrier to Ben Johnson's store and soon families gathered to mourn their loss. Ellen was buried at the north end of the potato field and folks returned to their homes.

Ely was devastated and looked as though he had aged ten years in three days. Angie was heart broken also but knew she had to be strong for her daddy. He had been her friend and protector all her life so she would be there for him now. She would mourn and grieve in private but now she would focus on keeping her daddy healthy and alive.

The spark that made the difference was a letter from Job that Ben Johnson had brought along to the funeral. Job had made it to Tuscaloosa, collected the reward money then moved on to the West. She had shared the letter with Ely and it seemed to revive his spirit.

She tucked the letter in her bosom next to her heart and kept it at arms reach by her bed at night. She had written a dozen letters to Job just waiting to receive an address from him. She had packed and repacked her trunk a dozen times in her mind. Every night before retiring to bed, she gazed into the black star filled sky and whispered a prayer for Job's safety and would repeat what her Mother had assured her of, "love will find a way!"

CHAPTER 18

THE TWO DOLLAR SHOOTOUT

A cool humid northeast wind had made life miserable for the past ten days but it had kept the wagon trail hard and dry. Big Miller and Spike were excellent wagon masters that kept the axles greased and harnesses in shape come rain or shine. Several times the big wagons had slipped into old water filled wagon ruts but they had pulled out of them all without breaking an axle or having to unload the wagon. The monotony and routine of trudging along at 10 miles a day had everyone's patience worn thin. The wagons were so bumpy and rough passing over the rough trail that the women and children walked most of the time.

It was now early spring in the Deep South and the subtle changes could be seen in the wet bottoms where the hardwoods were budding. They had deliberately bypassed the stores and a few villages along the way, knowing the thieves and highwaymen hung out around public places. Hearing about the high prices for food staples on the trail, they had stocked up on supplies in Jackson.

One thing Job was hoping to avoid was the so called trespass levy imposed by landowners on the trail south. The local landowners had built log bridges over the often flooded creeks and bayous and charged a fee to pass over them. Thieves and highwaymen had taken advantage of the prospect and laid claim to certain crossings in the road and charged as much as five dollars a wagon to cross over the bridge. The normal fee was a dollar per wagon that was accepted by travelers passing through.

Five dollars a wagon times two equaled a month's wages in the saw mills so Job had no intention of paying such a ridiculous fee. Folks could not wait for the flood waters to recede because the same five dollar fee applied to camping. The true ownership of the property at the crossing was questionable but any disagreement would lead to gunplay so most travelers forked over the fee. Those that were short on cash usually paid with livestock or family heirlooms. There were rumors of the women being taken advantage of to satisfy the toll. Job would pay the normal fee of a dollar per wagon but Hell would freeze over before he paid a month's wages to cross a swollen creek. He had spent days thinking over such incidents so he had a plan.

The creeks and bayous got deeper as they got closer to the Mississippi flood plain. At the deeper crossings they would chink the wagon beds with pieces of rag and moss to gain a little flotation for the wagons. They would ferry the women and children across on the extra horses, then Job would tie a rope to the lead mule on the first wagon to help pull if a wagon tried to swamp. By being careful and exercising safety measures, they had lost no wagon or injured anyone so far.

Two days out of Natchez their luck ran out on the trespass levy. By word of mouth they knew the deepest and most dangerous bayou crossing was ahead and it was run by hooligans. They had paid the two dollar levy at a crossing two days ago and the folks there had been kind enough to allow them to camp and use their cistern for good clean water.

There was a fork in the trail ahead and two crossings run by riff raff out of Natchez. Job knew both crossings were in cahoots and if you rejected one, the other would be even higher. Rumor had it that there had been bloodshed in the past so Job was ready for the worst.

The wagon train was in sight of the bayou crossing so Job decided it was time to have a serious talk with Big Miller and Spike. He halted the wagon train and dismounted calling the two men in for a powwow. He wanted to be discreet as to not frighten the women. He would be plain and straight forward and lay the law down on what they were facing.

"We are facing the last big crossing before Natchez. From what we've heard, I'd say the men running the crossing plan to rob us in plain daylight and make us like it. Now I don't figure on paying nobody a month's wages to cross their bridge. I'll offer up to two dollars a wagon to cross but that's it!" Job had stopped talking and tried to put on the most serious look he could. He laid the cards on the table.

"Now, if push comes to shove and I have to draw down on them fellers, I need you boys to do what I say and be pronto about it. If you got any other ideas, let's hear 'em." Job finished and scanned the farmer's faces for any doubt.

Both men nodded in anxious agreement then Big Miller spoke, "We got your back Job!" as he reached to reposition his gun and holster.

"All for one and one for all!" Spike was quick to agree.

Job continued, "We'll offer them a fair price but if they insist on chargin' an arm and a leg, we'll find another crossing."

Job felt better now that they had agreed. He instructed the women and children to walk out of sight behind the wagons and do exactly as told if trouble arose. Big Miller asked if he could offer a prayer for safety and Job removed his hat. He didn't understand it but the next few moments, while the farmers were praying he felt a strength and confidence overwhelm him. He shot a glance at Big Miller and the man gave him a knowing grin.

Everyone was in place and Job headed the wagons and moved them out. He chose the crossing to the left and downstream from the first crossing. There were two young men manning the bridge and they strolled to the middle of the trail as Job rode up and halted the wagons.

"Hidy Mister!" a young rough looking man carrying an old muzzle loader greeted them.

"Howdy!" Job responded and tipped his hat leisurely.

"You folks aiming to cross here for Natchez?" he asked.

"Yep if that's possible. What's the fee?" Job inquired.

"Two wagons and them extry horses will be ten dollars, Mister," the man said grinning like he knew they wouldn't like it.

Job whistled long and low looking about at both crossings and then downstream. The young man was eyeballin' the pistols in plain view on the team drivers and Job could tell it made him nervous.

"Ten dollars! That's a month's wages! We can't pay that. I'll give you two dollars a wagon Mister." Job replied and spat on the road.

"Ten dollars or you don't cross!" the man responded nasty like.

"At that rate we'll just have to make our own crossing downstream." Job replied calmly but matter of factly.

"You can't do that! This is ours and you gonna pay to use it!" the young man shot back in response then raised the long Tom waist level to make his point.

Job eased his hand to his pistol butt and replied, "Unless you can show me a deed and a land line, we gonna be moving downstream and crossing there. Now I'll give you two dollars a wagon and that's final!" He shifted his weight in the saddle to get ready to move quickly if needed.

The man with the rifle took a step toward Job's mule in anger and the other boy stepped up beside him. To Job's surprise he was carrying an old axe handle instead of a gun.

"You a smart one, ain't ye." The man sneered at Job and started to raise the rifle and point it at Job.

"You point that Tom at me and I'll take it as a threat mister!" Job declared loudly.

The man never hesitated at Job's warning but brought the rifle to his shoulder and was throwing the barrel down on Job when in one smooth motion he drew his .44 while cocking it at the same time. Pop had told him to strike while the iron was hot.

He fired at the man's leg striking him above the knee. All hell broke loose as he fell screaming to the ground. The men from the other crossing began yelling and cursing and the women and children were crying behind the wagons.

Job turned to Big Miller and screamed, "Move 'em across! Don't stop for a mile on the other side. Move! Move!"

He reined the mule between the wagons and the other crossing waving the pistol as a threat to the others.

The wounded man on the ground had passed out and the boy was pressing a rag on the wound. The men at the other crossing had not made a move to help their sidekicks so Job figured they were used to buffaloing people and cowards at heart. The wagons were over the bridge in five minutes and out of sight down the trail. Job took two dollars and threw it into the dirt beside the wounded man.

"I'm charging you two dollars for that slug in your partner's leg, there's the other two!" Job scowled at the man in the dirt, turned and rode over the bridge. There was a lot of shouting and commotion behind him as he rode out of sight.

The adrenalin was flowing and Job's mind was racing ninety to nothing. He had never shot a man before and he didn't like the feeling. He knew the men at the crossing planned to hijack them or maybe worse so he felt better knowing he had protected the women and children. He rode a while then stopped to listen for pursuers. He caught up to the wagons

101

ten minutes later. It was a pitiful sight, for the women and children's faces were streaked with dust and tears. The wagons stopped and Job rode up to Big Miller.

"Cut throats Big! I left 'em two dollars in the dirt. I doubt they'll follow us. The one I shot was hurt pretty bad, but he'll live." Job was still excited and talking made him feel better.

"That idiot drew down on you Job, I'd a done the same thing!" Big Miller said, sensing Job's anxiety over the shooting.

"Thanks Big." Job felt better hearing what he said.

Suddenly, Mrs. Miller's head appeared over Big's shoulder and she said, "Job you could have killed that man and we know that. You did only what you had to do and I think God saw that too. Thank you for keeping our children safe." There were tears on her face as she finished speaking.

Job was absolutely speechless but it was like a clean, cool wind in what she said. He tipped his hat at the women and rode ahead.

Turning in the saddle, he shouted to Big, "Let's try and find a safe place to camp before dark." He then rode back down the trail behind the wagons to listen for pursuers. There would be no pursuers, for the scallywags at the crossing had finally met a man of his word and they had no idea what to do with him.

CHAPTER 19

TWISTER!

The day after the two dollar shootout, as Big Miller called it now, the first spring storm roared through the Mississippi delta. The rain blew horizontal and from different directions at times. The wagons were pulled into a clearing away from the big timber. There was a roar and a wind like no one had ever seen before. The air was filled with leaves, tree limbs and sand. Job had dismounted and took shelter inside Big's canvas covered wagon. The water beneath the wagons was a foot deep and running down the trail into the creek that crossed the trail. They could only wait out the storm and hope for the best. The storm blew for three hours and then suddenly it was over. The sun came out and it was like a steam bath on the trail. Everyone unloaded from the wagons and began to hang everything out to dry.

The men had been watching the creek ahead as it had risen a foot an hour. They thought it best to cross the creek before dark and see how the trail would hold up further along. The wagons eased forward in the muck and mire and Job rode into the creek to check the bottom. The creek was passable but not for long. The water was becoming darker and heavier with silt by the minute. Job waved the wagons forward, they rolled into the swift water and passed over the creek without any trouble. In another hour, the creek would be impassable.

The wagon train was halted so everyone could get down and stretch their legs and dry out a bit. Everything was in good shape except for a couple of tears in the canvas wagon covers. The tears would be mended and the axles checked for mud and sand at the next camp. In an hour the wagons were on the move again. By looking at the sky, you could not prove there had been a violent storm overhead two hours ago.

Less than two miles down the trail they topped a small hill and what lay before them was beyond description. As far as the eye could see there was devastation and destruction. Whole trees were pulled up from the earth and laid on top of the ground. Other huge trees had been broken and twisted like kindling and thrown in every direction. Job had heard of these storms called twisters but had thought the stories were far fetched. He now saw first hand an act of God and boy did he have a story to tell. Everyone just sat and observed the destruction without a word spoken for five minutes.

The day was well spent so Job decided to camp so they could assess the trail ahead.

"Big! Spike! Maybe we ought to pitch camp here tonight so we can scout the trail ahead and find a way through this mess?" Job offered his advice to the others.

"You're right Job. Everybody's tuckered out and half drowned anyway." Spike agreed quickly.

"I'd like to take another day to mend these tarps and check these wagons out real good before we get to Natchez. We can get wagon parts and see a smitty if need be," Big Miller added wanting Job's final word.

"Good idea!" Job saw the wisdom in the suggestion.

"In that case I'm gonna whip up a big supper and sleep late tomorrow." Mrs. Miller chimed in. Everyone laughed because they knew she was always up before the rooster crowed.

Job scouted out a trail through the downed timber and rode back to camp before dark. He could smell the potatoes before he saw the wagons. Everyone needed a good rest and he planned on writing another letter to Angie and Pop so he could post it in Natchez. He couldn't wait to someday send an address so he could catch up on the news back home and most of all, hear from Angie. He knew he could strike out on his own and be in Texas in half the time. Lately he was realizing there was a great advantage in numbers on the wilderness trail. These were good strong people with backbones and they treated him like family. He was going to see them through to Texas.

The night watches went without incident and everyone rested well. Job rode further up the devastated trail the next morning and shot three rabbits for dinner. The twister had touched down for a quarter mile and then lifted. There were pine needles driven into tree trunks like porcupine quills and not far away the ground cover was not disturbed. Job wanted no beef with whoever controlled a storm like this. He was glad to be traveling with praying people.

The wagon train was ready to roll the next morning at the first light of day. Everyone was in good spirits and joking with one another.

Job had grabbed a biscuit, poked a hole in it and filled it with wild honey. He chased the last bite down with a big gulp of the black coffee. Nothing was wasted on the trail and everyone drank and ate till it was all gone.

Job rode out ahead to lead the wagons through the downed timber and debris that covered the trace. An hour later they were on the clear road and back to dodging the pot holes and wallows. They were hoping to arrive on the edge of Natchez by evening and everyone was so excited. There were pig trails and wagon trails leading in to the trace from other directions now and they were overtaking other travelers.

There were a lot of hellos and information passed between the travelers but no one stopped to gab. A U.S. Army patrol was riding north from Natchez to survey the twister damage and open the trace where trees had blocked the road. The Natchez Trace was now a U.S. government claimed jurisdiction of the trace as a matter of national defense and kept the road open year round.

By late afternoon the wagon train was two miles from Natchez and the ferry crossing. From a passerby Job learned it was slow season at the ferry but was still a four hour wait in line to pass over the river. Jackson had been a mess of hustle and bustle but Natchez was a log jam of commerce. Job talked it over with the men and decided to pull into the ferry line and wait it out if it took all night. The ferry would run all night in the moonlight as long as the river was not at flood level. They could take cat naps waiting in line and re-supply and rest up on the Louisiana side the next day.

At four am that night, Job's party boarded the ferry and took the one hour ride across the mighty Mississippi. They were west of the Mississippi now and everyone considered themselves pioneers and they were excited. This was a milestone in Job's adventure and he had written extra long letters to Angie and Pop. During the long wait in line for the ferry, he had posted everyone's mail and also did a little purchasing of vitals. He bought a half dozen tobacco plugs for himself and several tobacco twists for the mule. The lady folks and children were thrilled with the rock candy he bought for them.

Job noticed people gave him plenty of space in town and didn't know if it was his pistol contraption or Indian looks. The ferry master looked as though he wanted to say something as Job led his mule onto the ferry. The man had noticed that Job was the overseer of the wagons following him and said nothing. After they boarded, Spike pointed at a faded crude sign tacked to a ferry rail. "No Injuns and Aferkans must be in irons."

The river crossing went well enough and streaks of daylight were painting the cold eastern sky when the wagons pulled onto Louisiana soil. They had decided on another day of rest and re-supply. Job inquired of an Army sentry of what lay ahead on the trail.

"You can pull up outside Vidalia and rest. Jest don't stop on no plantation property or give nuthin' to the Aferkans. The trail to Alexandria is plain marked and don't git off of it." He instructed.

The soldier admired the mules and horses then continues, "From here on out, forget your wife and sleep with yore mule. That mule is worth a fortune in these parts." He grinned and Job thanked him.

An hour after daybreak, Job pulled the wagon train up outside the town of Vidalia. There were several blacksmith and cooper shops along the dirt road. Most places looked well used and permanent so Job figured the local plantations were serviced by these places. No one paid much attention to another wagon train passing through except for the keen eyes of the locals looking over their livestock. Job was not going to be caught with his britches down and took the warning about the mules and horses to heart. He had a few tricks to keep the horse thieves at bay and would explain them to the others later.

Everyone was tired and sleepy after the all night ferry crossing. The children had slept through most of the crossing and were wide awake and adventurous. The adults would take turns catching up on their sleep. Being so close to town afforded no privacy but they were able to purchase grease for their wagon axles and check the wagons over. A fish seller came by and the ladies decided to have a fish fry. The peddler skinned and cleaned the catfish for one dollar. The man had built a water tight live box from cypress. Folks could pick their fish fresh daily and he would clean them on the wagon's tail board. The peddler informed them they were about five days ride by wagon from Alexandria, La and two weeks to the Sabine River crossing at Gaines Ferry.

While the ladies fried the fish, the men finished fine tuning the repairs on the wagons and tarps. A local parson stopped by and visited a while. He shared the common information on the trail ahead and cautioned them not to trespass on the plantations. He said it was wise not to even express your opinion on slavery in these parts.

The parson offered a prayer for their safety and everyone felt better from his expression of kindness.

Job wondered about his advice on keeping silent about such a passionate issue as slavery. Just like the Indian problem, slavery would never be abolished until people were informed and it was spoken against. He would take it one day at a time and the situation would warrant whether he would be silent.

CHAPTER 20

ALEC' AND

THE LESSON IN MANNERS

The first day of March found the wagon train a days ride from Alexandria, La. The past four days had been uneventful except for the spring thunderstorms that seemed to pop up without warning. The cold rain was refreshing but the sultry sauna that followed was miserable. There seemed to be no wind at times and the bugs grew in number daily. The deer flies and the horse flies tormented the livestock and people. The mosquitoes at night were almost unbearable. Several fires would be built and smothered to create a smoke to drive the bugs away. The ladies tied up bedspreads to sleep under and everyone slept wet with sweat. The cooking lard smeared on the arms and neck helped in the daylight but red welts covered everyone. Finding a high place in a clearing meant less mosquitoes at night but those campsites were far apart.

The wagon road they were following along had meandered along the outskirts of the plantations and were aimed at the shallow crossings of creeks and bayous. The travelers got an occasional glimpse of the field workers and would pass a ragtag group moving from one field to another. The slaves would be singing the most haunting and beautiful songs as they labored. They reminded Job of the great spiritual songs of the Cherokee. Their songs would tell a story of a hunt, a death or battle fought. Tribal history was kept alive through songs and great truths revealed to each new generation. You could feel the anguish and heartache in the tone of the singing slaves.

The band of travelers hoped to reach the banks of the Red River by dark and camp before entering town. From other travelers they had learned there were shallow crossings at the river but very swift and dangerous rapids. They would have to detour several miles around the rapids to cross safely. They reached the river in the late afternoon and traveled its bank for two miles to the north before making camp. There were campers nearby and they settled in a small clearing in sight of the river. There was a nice breeze coming off the river and everyone felt better as they made camp.

Job's strategy of self defense had kept the horse thieves and bushwhackers at bay.

"Speak softly but carry a big stick." The philosophy his Pop had instilled in him had proven true time and again.

Job's wagon train was a tight knit and self sufficient group now and everyone had their duties and knew their place. Since the two dollar shootout, Job had given the men and ladies lessons and target practice with the pistols. To survive out West, the women must learn to shoot and to defend their families.

The next day was Sunday so the men decided to make a late crossing of the Red River. The ladies were up at daybreak stirring up breakfast as the men cinched and tightened everything for the river crossing before noon. Job saddled Red and rode to the crossing to watch a couple of wagons pass over the river. The river was shallow and swift with no need of caulking the wagons. He rode into the river and up the west bank. He felt so good after crossing the river, he let out a yell then waved back at everyone on the east side. The grownups stopped to wave back and all the children ran to the edge of the bank to yell and carry on. They had reached a milestone and Job's pleasure was shared by everyone.

Back in camp, everyone had a good breakfast and Big Miller broke out the Good Book for the reading and a prayer of Thanksgiving. His mention of Job as being their "Joshua" tickled the children and that would be his moniker for days to come. He was deeply humbled by the love he felt from these folks and deep in his heart he gave thanks to the Great Spirit for such good fortune. The only thing missing was Angie being beside him for the rest of his life. For some reason he felt a foreboding and urgency to hear from her. He felt a pain for her that was new and wondered if all was well on the Cooper farm. With tear filled eyes he whispered a silent prayer that the Great Spirit would keep her and hasten their reunion.

The river crossing went well and before noon the wagon train was on the west side of Alec' as the locals called it. The passage through town was not as crowded as Natchez had been but Job noticed a wildness that gripped the place. The further west of the Mississippi River they traveled, the less civilized it became. There was an intimidation factor at play on the trail through town and more than once Job had actually drew his pistol to share the right of way with the freight wagons.

Big Miller had actually bailed off his wagon seat after a mule skinner that had cussed at him for having to detour around his wagon. The man fled off down the trail and Big gave up the chase.

His comment was, "You gonna respect the ladies and chillin' or learn some manners the hard way!"

Mrs. Miller consoled him and wiped his red face as she tried to calm him down. Job didn't know what to say but then Spike began to laugh and mimic the mule skinner fleeing from the wrath of Big Miller.

"He beat that poor ole mule he was riding nearly to death trying to out run you Big!" he said smiling.

"Well that wadn't very Christian of me to fly off the handle like that but I won't tolerate no filthy mouth talkin' around my missus and chillin'!" Big tried to justify his actions as the wagons pulled ahead. The children had a new character to imitate now as they replayed their daddy chasing the mule skinner down the dirt road. The laughter helped everyone feel better as Job halted the wagons at a large dry goods store and post office on the edge of town. He remembered a saying of his mother that just played itself out, "Laughter is good for the soul."

His daddy's words rang out in his head, "A sense of humor will go a long way in life. It will even temper death!"

They were going to need all the help they could get to survive where they were going, Job thought.

The men took their purchases in the store and the ladies followed. The prices were higher the farther they got from the Mississippi River.

Job posted a letter to Angie, Pop, and the Halls. He told them his destination was Nacogdoches, Texas and to post his mail to that address. He figured they would cross the Sabine River by the last week of March and that Nacogdoches would be his base camp for future correspondence.

The storekeep said they were a hundred miles from the Sabine River. He spoke to Big Miller and never acknowledged Job's presence.

"You get some protection from the law close to town but watch for outlaws and thievin' Injuns the further out you get." He emphasized the Indian part and cast a sarcastic glance at Job.

"You sayin' a white man stealing from you is better than an Indian stealin' from you?" Job shot back.

The clerk was taken aback that Job would even speak to a white man in public and marveled at his perfect English.

"You know what I mean, so get your grub and get out!" he said as he reached beneath the counter.

Job had his hand on his pistol as he turned and walked out with Big and Spike at his back.

"They treat you like you half naked and wearing a war bonnet!" Spike said chuckling as they reached the wagons.

"Yeah, I may be more trouble to you folks than I'm worth." Job said apologetically while packing his provisions away.

Big Miller cut Job off quickly saying, "Hey, that man is as ignorant as an ass! The only thing that's gonna change folks like that is us walking together, eatin' together and standing back to back thru hell and high water! The Almighty made color, He likes it, so who am I to argue?" Big slapped Job on the back as he finished his say. Job felt better and grinned with relief.

Besides his in-laws, he had never known such civil and tolerant white people.

It was Spikes turn and he always had something practical and amusing to say about every situation.

"What gets me is we all eat an egg out of a chicken's butt, we bleed red, cry tears, squat down to crap and all look alike save for skin color and want to hate each other over one difference." Spike finished his lecture almost out of breath.

"With your perspective on things and clear way of puttin' it, you ought to run for President, Spike," Big pitched in agreeing to his assessment.

"Nope, wouldn't live to see my next birthday. Somebody shoot me before I got elected." Spike rejected the offer of nomination.

They got their provisions packed away and now the ladies could take their turn in the store. Big accompanied the ladies after Job's spat with the clerk. He would not allow no disrespect of the ladies for their keeping company with Job. The ladies thought it odd that Big come along but he never clued them in to what had been said.

Growing up, Big's mother had told him often, "Try not to puke in public." As he grew older he saw the wisdom in what she was teaching him. Some things are better not publicized or repeated. Human nature always seeks out the negative and derogatory first. Big believed in nipping it in the bud. Things were kept a lot more pleasant that way.

The ladies were back with their provisions and Job headed the wagons out of Alec', west on to El Camino Real, the Old San Antonio Road.

This trail was by no means a road. The Natchez Trace was bad enough and kept open by federal troops. The Old San Antonio Road was just plain treacherous! To avoid the major wagon ruts, the traffic had spread out over time and the trail would be several acres wide at points. Job rode ahead and searched diligently for the best passage. He would break off a myrtle bush or a pine limb for the wagons to follow. It was hard work and slow going but travel did seem to get better the farther from town they got.

Job decided to pack it in a little early that evening to organize and plan for their night watch and clean up from the dusty ride through Alec'. The red dust that covered everyone from town was half animal waste and the smell was sickening. Job had picked out an open space beside the creek and waited on the wagons to catch up. He had taken a raccoon bath before they arrived and was building a fire when they pulled into the camp. The ladies and kids were so glad to be stopping early. The trail had been so rough that they had walked several miles over the rough terrain. Job knew there would be taters and onions for supper and that might have figured into his decision for an early camp.

CHAPTER 21

CADDO

The last three days had been tough but the little wagon train had averaged 12-15 miles per day. Spring was in full bloom and the weather was unpredictable from morning till evening. The warm days not only brought new grass for the livestock but hoards of mosquitoes, gnats, deer and horse flies. The gnats would fill your eyes and fly up your nose and into your ears. Everyone was wearing a bandana over their mouth and bits of cloth stuffed in their ears. The high ground was not so bad but the creek bottoms were torment. The occasional breeze that accompanied the thunderstorms was a great relief.

The plan was to follow the Old San Antonio trail northwest to a small town called Natchitoches, which lay north of the military outpost of Fort Jessup. From this, the trail continued another fifty miles to Gaines Ferry on the Sabine River. They would cross the river and continue to Nacogdoches, Texas another three days ride west. This large town was a trading post and major hub of commerce for the cattle drives and pioneers heading south to Mexico or west to California and the Oregon territories. They would set up camp close to town and plan their next move. Job hoped to find work in the lumber mills or freighting down the Sabine River. The steam boats were offloading and picking up cotton, lumber and dry goods at a dozen stops on the trip south to Sabine Pass on the Gulf of Mexico. Job was a jack of all trades and a master of several. Fifty cents a day plus supper in a peck mill sounded pretty good to him. Every day closer to Texas was a day closer to Angie. He couldn't help but to perk up at the thought of a new start in Texas with Angie at his side. He swatted another fly and pushed on down the trail.

A mail rider out of Natchitoches informed them they were a day's ride from town. He said the trail west was in fair condition with an occasional creek out of banks that run off in a day. Letter mail was averaging thirty days from Nacogdoches, Texas to Atlanta Georgia. The carrier was a Carolina boy like Big and Spike so he said he would bend the rules a little and take their letters back east. The kind favor would hasten their delivery by at least a month and everyone was excited about that. Everyone included Nacogdoches, Texas as a temporary address to receive their mail.

Camp was made early that evening so a tally of provisions could be made and the harness and wagon hubs checked. They would stop in town only for provisions. The Sabine River crossing and Texas was on everybody's mind and excitement was in the air. Spike made a sweep up the creek next to the camp, shot six times and came back with four rabbits. There would be fried rabbit with red eye gravy for supper. Mrs. Miller was patting out cat head biscuits to sop the gravy and wild honey.

A low rumble of thunder could be heard in the southeast and Job figured they were in for a thunderstorm after dark. Everyone was entertained by the lightening display till bedtime. Job took up his night watch at midnight and the rain came around two am in the morning. The storm was mostly wind and died down before daylight.

The campers were rolling up and shaking water out of everything when Spike hollered for Job and Big where the livestock were hobbled.

"Blue's gone! The hobble is not even here. He didn't wander off, he was taken!" Spike was breathless over the loss of their best riding horse.

Job made a search for the tracks around the camp and came up with an occasional horse track in the direction of town. The rain had almost covered the trail but an experienced woodsman like Job could see the spaced out puddles of water that only a horse or mule track would make. Back in camp Job gave instructions to Big and Spike. Time was crucial and he had to move quickly.

"Move on to Natchitoches and camp on the west side of town! Don't wait over one day for me. Make for the Sabine River at Gaines Ferry and then to Nacogdoches. I'll probably catch you way before then but don't hold up for me!" Job was saddling Red and checking his weapon while he barked instructions. Big had filled his canteen and handed him a couple of leftover biscuits wrapped in old news print. He mounted Red and was off in minutes. One of the children yelled after him, "Go get 'em Joshua!" He waved and rode out of sight.

A horse like Blue would fetch a year's wages in these parts and men would kill for such a fine animal. Spike had branded a crude S on the animal's left flank and showed Job another marking in the horse's ear he could recognize if the need ever arose.

Job followed the tracks for over a mile and then the trail turned north along a white oak hammock and solid ground. The thief steered clear of soft spots and low places so not to leave tracks and Job knew this was no novice. There was never a heel or boot print where the thief dismounted and Job's suspicion grew of the kind of thief he was tracking. The man was either a hunter or an Indian! The horse was being lead or ridden over the root systems and only hard ground to minimize tracks. There was never spittle or piss for a clue. He had figured out the thief's strategy and it was exactly how he would throw a pursuer!

Job pressed Red to a trot and was more than three miles from camp still heading due north. A thief of this caliber would be cautious but confident in his ability to cover his trail. Maybe over confident, thought Job. Pop had warned him that being over confident would lead to mistakes. Sure enough, the thief grew careless an hour later. Job noticed a gum bud had been nibbled. The thief had paused here for some reason so Job scouted around for more signs. The man had found a hollow tree and pissed inside the hollow to conceal the smell. From the sharp stench, Job knew his man was no more than an hour away.

Job continued his pace but stayed tuned in to his surroundings. Thirty minutes later a Hinny Penny began to chatter a hundred yards ahead. The adrenaline began to flow and his senses intensified as he dismounted and tied Red to a sapling. He felt he needed to go forward on foot. His instincts had always served him well. Job crept from tree to tree listening to the wind and forest sounds. The Hinny Penny had stopped chattering then Job heard the faint clink of metal against metal.

There was a rise in the terrain ahead and what looked like a hickory stand of timber. The perfect place for a camp and high ground to keep watch all around. There must be water nearby, thought Job, so he circled the grove to the east and found a branch that seeped from the small hill. He worked his way up the branch, sometimes crawling through the thicket till he reached the hickory grove. In the grove was a pole wigwam and a meat rack beside it and a small plume of smoke rising through the rack.

The draft in the clearing was pulling the smoke straight up and that's why he had never smelled anything.

There was no activity in the camp but Job saw a small Indian man kneeling beside an Indian girl holding what looked like a baby. A deep dread gripped Job's conscience seeing the woman and the baby. He knew he had to retrieve the stolen horse but he didn't know if he could pull it off without violence. He had to get it done before the dread overcome his better sense. Working his way low to the ground and tree to tree, he got within a hundred feet of the camp without being noticed. The Indian man was caught up in playing with the baby.

Job approached the man from behind and neither person saw him till he spoke.

"Ho!" Job spoke sharply and loud with his .44 pointed at the man's back. The feller whirled and reached for a skinning knife at his waist till he saw Job's pistol and froze. The woman began to cry and conceal her baby. The man was Job's age, short, squatty and dark complexion. Job knew from reading history books that there was a Caddo Indian clan in this area before their displacement north of the Red River.

Job motioned the man to toss the knife away and to sit on the ground. He then pointed at Blue tied next to the wigwam. He made a S sign in the air then pointed to his hip and the horse's. He then tapped his chest and simply said, "Mine!"

The young man hung his head in defeat and waited for the worse to happen. His young wife began to wail louder. They both knew the penalty for horse stealing. Job reached inside his shirt and pulled out the tribal token and let it fall onto his chest. The young woman grew big eyed and spoke to her husband sharply. He raised his eyes to Job's chest and seemed to relax a little.

Job gave the universal hand signal of the Indian clans and spoke, "Cherokee!" tapping his chest as he spoke.

The man nodded and placing his palm on his chest replied, "Caddo."

Job continued speaking in English, "You steal. Mine." He pointed at Blue again.

The young brave only nodded and pointed north. He spoke in broken English, "Red River . . . all Caddo . . . no food . . . sick . . . I come back . . . family." He pointed at his wife and newborn baby, and hung his head again in shame.

Job fully understood the plight of the young Indian couple. Rather than stay north of the Red River in poverty and disease, the brave young man had chosen to take a chance on surviving in the ancient tribal land of the Caddo which the white men had stolen.

The young Caddo brave never lifted his eyes when he spoke, "No steal horse! Find . . . on trail . . . big storm . . . great light!"

Job had trouble believing what he was hearing. They had read the sign wrong and had overlooked something in the camp. There was just something about this young man that made Job believe him.

"Good! No problem!" Job replied. "I take horse and go." He kept his pistol drawn and walked to Blue and untied him. Leading him back to where the couple sat on the ground, he stopped and spoke.

"Trouble here, go north, Caddo land!" Job tried to emphasize the danger in these parts for an Indian.

The brave looked up with fire in his eyes, shook his head no and said, "Stay, Caddo land."

Job could see he was wasting his time. He noticed how poor their camp was and reached into his pocket for a four bit piece and into his ammo pouch for several pieces of rock candy he kept there. He carefully squatted and laid the silver coin and candy before the young man and rose to leave.

The surprise was evident on the faces of both the young people. Tears streamed down the young woman's face and she smiled at Job briefly. He knew what was next as the Caddo brave reached into a pouch at his waist and brought out a very handsome and never used arrow head. Hours had been spent chipping and toiling over the flint to perfect the head. He offered it up to Job and Job received the gift. He motioned the young man to rise and extended his hand for the traditional hand clasp. The young man was deeply moved by such great respect for him in the presence of his wife. He blessed Job in the Caddo tongue, Job turned and left their camp. He back tracked where Red was tied and was back on the wagon train an hour later.

There was celebrating in the camp because all had went well and Job was safe. Soon after Job had left that morning in pursuit of the thief, Big Miller had found Blue's hobble close by and it had been pulled loose. Job related the Caddo brave's story and everyone was amazed. Someone could have been accidentally killed over the matter and Job had never been so relieved and happy in his life. His parents teaching about not reacting in anger and a hasty spirit, had served him well again.

Too much had happened that morning to move camp and pass through Natchitoches, so they would spend another night where they were. The ladies decided to fry up Job's favorite, taters and onions, to celebrate their good fortune. Job slept well that night, with his onion breath and dreams of Angie and Texas on his mind.

CHAPTER 22

GAINES FERRY AND TEXAS

The passage through Natchitoches the next day went without incident. The wagons made a stop at the dry goods for potatoes and a sack of salt. Job replenished his chewing tobacco for himself and the mule and bought a sack of rock candy for the kids and his enjoyment. There was not a wave or so much as a nod at Job as he rode ahead of the wagons through town. Ignorance and intolerance was at a premium the further west he traveled, thought Job. He probably would have been bushwhacked long ago if not in the company of Big and Spike. Their outfit was a formidable sight to see with their fancy but practical holstered weapons and fine wagons. Their healthy animals were worth their weight in gold out here.

A days ride west of town they met a Calvary patrol from Fort Jessup and caught up on the news from Texas and back east.

The Lieutenant kept an eye on Job as the men talked. He finally could not hold his curiosity no longer and asked Job, "You Injun or Mexkin?" He spoke in an official tone and a tense silence followed.

Job never batted an eye in response, "Mother was Cherokee. I got papers showing that I'm an American citizen." He patted his saddle bag indicating proof.

"Could I have a look-see?" the officer asked.

Job brought out his birth certificate showing his Caucasian Father and handed them to the officer. He took his time looking them over and passed them back.

"Stay close to these white folks when you cross the river. They's folks over there that will shoot and ask questions later!" he advised Job.

The party exchanged pleasantries and moved on their way.

"Maybe I need to shave ny head." Job remarked as they rode away.

"Wouldn't do you any good with that nose and those eyes," Spike said, grinning at Job.

Big Miller put in his two cents worth. "Keep your chin up, them papers handy and let us worry about your back." He encouraged Job wisely.

Spring had sprung in these parts. The next three days was toil as the wagons dodged other traveler's ands the treacherous wagon ruts full of water. They stopped to help a family whose wagon was almost on its side in a rut. Nothing was broken but it took two mules and all the men to shove the wagon out of the deep mire. The man, Ike Wills, was a blacksmith and cooper and his wife, Jane, and three teenagers were from Georgia. They war resettling in Texas and asked to join Job's train. The more the merrier was Big's philosophy. He explained that Job was the trail boss and had final say for the group. Everyone shook hands and visited while cleaning the mud from their hands and feet.

Two rough and tough days later they were a mile from the Sabine River and Texas! Wagon traffic had come to a halt. The river was on a rise and it would take a full day of stop and go to cross the river. When the river was low, the foot traffic could cross the river at a sand bar in a bend below the ferry. With the river rising, there were suck holes and shifting sand and too dangerous to swim.

Gaines Ferry had its hawkers, hooligans and bums. A medicine man was peddling his brew and a bootlegger was selling white lightening and corn liquor. Job's train kept its place in line and visited with their new family. Most traffic coming out of Texas were freighters and never stopped long enough to visit. The river crossing was a little turbulent but Job's train made it without any trouble. There was a cluster of buildings and sheds at the steamboat stop on the west bank and the wagons had to work their way through the small town. An hour west of the river was a creek crossing and camp was made before dark.

Big Miller had bought twenty pounds of catfish, tote sack and all from a peddler and they went about skinning the fish for supper. Job rode down the trail for another mile for a little privacy and to take care of a man's business. He was overjoyed to be standing on Texas soil and wondered if Angie would sense his pleasure and love for her at the moment. He could smell the catfish frying a hundred yards from camp on his way back and the laughter and conversation around the fire made him lovesick for Angie's company. He was a day closer to her and in Texas. He would look up and be patient, his day would come.

The new family introduced themselves formally around the supper fire that evening. Ike and Jane Wills had two teenage sons, Jack and James, and a teenage daughter, Grace. The "go west" bug had bitten them and they had left a farm and a struggling smith shop in southwest Georgia. Ike said the mail order catalogs had taken much of his tool and plow business and rumor had it that a good blacksmith or cooper could fare well out west. Mrs. Wills was a school teacher so they figured their services would bring a premium in Texas. The Miller and Spike family was overjoyed to know that they had a certified school marm on board and they were already hoping they could all settle out west together to benefit one another. All they needed now was a preacher and a sheriff. One of the children piped up and elected Job as sheriff and everyone agreed and laughed. Before it was over, Spike had to tell the story of the two dollar shootout. By the time he had finished, Job was as famous as Stonewall Jackson.

The Wills had left Georgia before Christmas and had experienced a lot of setbacks on the way. They had paid the trespass fee of five dollars twice and chills and fever had stopped them for three days. What was so surprising was that they had spent the night at Johnson's Corner store and heard about the rescue of a beautiful white girl, by a Cherokee warrior, from a murdering white slaver. The incident had become legend now and Job laughed until his side hurt listening to Ike and the boys relate the story. They were a little taken aback by Job's antics and he apologized and clued them in on the truth. They were speechless after Job's version.

One of the boys burst out, "You are a real Cherokee Indian?"

His daddy hushed him but Job nodded and extended his hand. "Yep, just like you just a little more tan!" Everyone laughed and the conversation played out at bedtime.

Job walked off into the darkness and thought of how close the Wills family had come to the Cooper farm. Angie could have climbed onto their wagon and been here with him in the moonlight tonight. Tears filled his eyes and a longing gripped his heart as he looked up at the same moon she was probably watching.

Pop had had said that man's days were brief and full of trouble. Now Job was realizing and benefiting from his elders teachings everyday. He wondered how Pop was faring in Savannah and if he would ever see his beloved Grandfather again. Maybe he and Angie could take a stagecoach back east someday after they get settled in Texas. He didn't even have a place for Angie to lay her head and he was already taking vacations with her. Oh well, He thought, a man has to have a vision or he will perish. He remembered his Mother reading this out of the Good Book. His big imagination made him feel good and enabled him to put one foot ahead of the other each day. He felt privileged and blessed with such a bright future.

Their first night in Texas was pleasant and all the night watches were quiet. With the new family joined up, the men were able to break the watches into three hour shifts which made life a lot easier for all. Ike carried a new percussion rifle and knew how to use it. He also holstered what he called a Bowie knife that was big enough to beat a man to death with. He was interested in acquiring a pistol and set about fashioning a holster like the other men were wearing.

From fellers they met on the trail, they knew they were no more than four days ride from Nacogdoches, Texas. The next day at noon, the wagon train pulled into a trading post called Milam. It was a busy crossroad with a Post Office. Everyone took time to post a letter back East and to shop for necessities. Job bought his mule a strong twist of tobacco and a sassafras root to make tea that evening. He got a kick out of sharing his knowledge of herbs and remedies with the children. He would mix a little ground sassafras with the bear grease or lard they used on their heads and necks to keep the insects away. You could smell the wagon coming before you saw them. Anything was acceptable to help endure the mosquito and deer flies. Mrs. Wills was recording the cures and remedies that Job related and the questions were never ending. She hoped someday to publish her own almanac as a reference guide for the pioneers and farmers to use.

The postmaster at Milam said they were a good day's ride from another small town on the trail called San Augustine. The wagons pushed on until evening and a kind farmer allowed them to camp in his corn field. There was an open well which meant access to clean water. The farmer broke out popcorn and there was fun and games till dark. The children were put to bed and the men talked Texas for hours. The farmer advised them to push for the Angelina River to camp the next day. East Texas was already settled from the Sabine River West, a hundred miles beyond Nacogdoches. If they found a suitable campsite on the Angelina River, a man on horseback could make Nacogdoches in a full day of riding. They could register at the land office and check the want ads posted outside. A good hand could fetch a dollar a day on the cattle drives and steamboat docks on the Sabine River. The peck mills paid fifty cents a day plus a bowl of corn mush. The sky was the limits for smiths, coopers and leather workers.

Everyone went to bed excited and looking forward to seeing Nacogdoches. Camp broke at daylight and the farmer's wife surprised them with fried potato pone for breakfast. The farmer asked that they send word by mail carrier if they put together a wagon train to move further west. He felt crowded and was thinking of selling out and moving to Oregon territory.

The wagon train arrived on the Angelina River before noon that day. There were mule pens and several farms at the crossing. Big and Spike rode out to make arrangements with the local land owners to camp several days above the mule pens. Most folks were very hospitable and they were settled in and had wagons and riders stopping by till dark to visit. They were starving for news from back east. Some folks brought popcorn and hickory nuts and chinquapins to eat. Big Miller and Spike were offered a months work on busted wheels and plows.

Job rode out hunting every morning for fresh meat and bagged a nice spike buck the first day. This was beautiful and rich country and he could live right here with Angie, he thought. The local folks were a little cool in his presence but they had accepted him. His knowledge of leather, herbs and mules was superb. He stayed busy all day curing leather and answering questions from Mrs. Wills about herbs for medicine.

After three days, it was decided that Job and Big Miller would make the ride to Nacogdoches to gather information for the next move. Everyone knew it was too early but they wanted to check the mail and send off more letters. It was pleasant making the ride with Big the next day. The closer they got to Nacogdoches, the more crowded the trail became. Farmers, ranchers, frontiersmen and soldiers were like ants filtering in from every direction. Job had one thing on his mind and that was the post office! He knew it was a month too soon but this was a milestone in his quest and he cherished the hope it gave.

CHAPTER 23

LETTERS FROM TEXAS

A ngie and her daddy, Coop, had trudged on with life one day at a time after her Mother's passing. Potatoes had been planted and she had enjoyed the work for it kept her mind momentarily off of Job. It was the end of March and she was hoping for a letter any day.

Mr. Cooper was holding up but the life had gone out of his eyes. Angie saw him often weeping at his beloved's grave. She knew there had to be a change or she would lose her Daddy too. She couldn't bring herself to breech the subject of leaving the farm and Ellen's grave. She hoped and prayed a letter from Job would spark some interest in Texas for her Father. He loved Job and mentioned his name daily. He would even perk up a little when the mail carrier rode by.

The second week of April the hickory tree buds in the back yard had burst open into tender leaves. Coop had always declared that the hickory tree did not lie. Other trees would bud and leaf, the dogwood would leaf and flower and sometimes be caught by a killing frost. The wild plum and Indian peach grove had given up their precious and tender buds to a late frost often. When the hickory tree budded, spring had come, the hickory did not lie!

Coop had bedded plants in the potato shed for spring planting and they were two to four inches high. The tomato and squash were Angie's favorite. It was extra work but she would tenderly cover the young plants at night with myrtle bush branches and green pine limbs. The rabbits and deer did not like the turpentine smell and the cover kept the cooler nights from stunting the plants growth.

Angie was finishing up in the vegetable garden before dark on Saturday evening when Coop called her name from the well house. There was a different tone in his voice and she dropped everything to hurry and check on her Daddy. When she came from behind the potato shed, he was standing at the well with the biggest grin on his face that she hadn't seen since Ellen's death. He was holding several envelopes like they were expensive China cups. She lost her composure immediately as she rushed to Coop and cupped her hands over her daddy's holding the mail.

"Job?" was all she could mutter searching her daddy's face for hope.

"Yes baby! Four letters, three for you and he even wrote me and Ellen!" her father said.

"Oh daddy, let me wash my hands and make some coffee and we'll open them together!" she smiled through her tears of joy. Coop had never stopped grinning as they both tenderly clutched the letters in their hands together.

Angie rushed to cleanup and started the coffee. Coop was sitting at the kitchen table and they took Ellen's pen knife to open the letters. Angie took the paper and held it to her nose to capture any scent of Job. To her the letter smelled clean and her heart burst with joy. The letters had been posted in Meridian, Jackson and Natchez, Mississippi. She read through each one quickly then started over trying to live each line. He spoke of how close he felt to her watching the moon at night knowing she was gazing at the same time. He said at times I can smell your sweetness and it was so real. She laid her head on the kitchen table and the hot tears of joy wet the pages.

Coop had read his letter and reached over and patted her back.

"Angie, you alright?" he whispered.

"Yes daddy, I am now!" she replied.

"Here baby, I want you to read mine . . . mine and Ellen's letter." He said softly.

She took the letter and read it out loud as Coop listened.

"Mr. and Mrs. Cooper, I hope you are all well. I am fine and have made it as far as Jackson, Mississippi. I miss you both. Besides Pop, you are my family. Every thing I do now, is with you in mind and a future for your beloved daughter, Angie. I love her with all my being and every thing

I do is to prepare and secure a future for her with me. Please keep me in your prayers and I will see you someday. Job"

She squeezed Coop's hand and gave him back the letter.

"I've often wondered what it would be like to have a son and now I know. I know now and oh how Ellen would have loved to hear this!" he beamed with joy.

Coop's spirit was reviving at that moment and she could see the fire back in his eyes. It seemed he had other important things to say but refrained from doing so.

"Daddy, my last letter is from Natchez, Mississippi and Job has joined up with several other families heading west and he is the trail boss! He's probably in Texas by now and I can't wait for the next letter!" she said smiling.

"One day at a time, baby. It will happen. Love will find a way." He consoled his daughter.

"Why Daddy, Mother said those same words to me, love will find a way." She smiled as she finished her coffee.

"It was a motto that we lived by honey. Through thick and thin, love for one another has pulled us through. Now baby, I'm going out to read this to Ellen and I want you to come along. It's important that you be there." Coop was sober minded and she saw her daddy had passed from his terrible grief and come home to her.

"Sure daddy, it's almost dark, let me get a shawl and your coat." She said.

They made their way to Ellen's grave as the orange and blue sky outlined the tree tops.

Coop stood a moment in silence and then read Job's letter to him and Ellen. He broke a couple of times but finally finished.

He spoke with a deep sincerity and Angie felt like a farewell note rang through his trembling voice.

"Ellen darling, I've hung on here as long as I can with you. You know I got to do what's right by Angie. She's all I got in this world, besides Job. Ellen, honey . . . I don't know just when, but some day soon, I'm going to Texas with Angie." He stopped and looked at Angie's face in the dim evening light. She was big eyed but smiled at her daddy and shook her head, Yes!

She encouraged her daddy by saying, "It's what Job and I want daddy, it's the right thing to do and I know that mother is happy to hear that."

Angie hoped Job could sense the moment and somehow realize what she had just heard. The wheels were in motion and they were going to Texas! Her daddy always thought things through and would sleep on a decision before he made it public. She knew that every waking moment would be filled with preparation to leave for Texas. Her daddy had made his decision, slept on it and spoken. She didn't know what all was to follow at her young age but Coop had made her the happiest girl in the whole wide world! Love was finding a way.

Coop would never let Angie out of sight after her kidnapping and two days later he said they were riding in to Johnson's Corner for a few things. She prepared for a daylight departure and packed their lunch and water keg. The trip was wonderful in the spring weather. The dogwoods were in full bloom and the honey suckle were showing in a few places. The trail was filled with folks going places in the pleasant weather. They arrived at noon at the Johnson's store and bought a few sundries they needed. As usual, the Johnson's invited them to lunch and they talked and showed Job's letters over poke salad and sassafras tea.

Finally Coop revealed the intent of their trip to town, as he called it.

"Ben, Martha, I got an announcement to make and some business that I need your help with." He looked at Ben matter of factly.

"Why sure Coop, anything I can do to help." He offered.

"Well, I've thought it over for a couple of months and I've decided to sell the farm and go west to Texas." He finished and let the news soak in a while.

Ben and Martha looked at one another and he turned to Coop with a grin and said, "Coop there ain't a more sensible and level headed man in this county than you. I think I understand and I'm with you. I just hate to lose a friend and neighbor like you and Angie." He finished and hugged Martha as she began to cry. They had all been through so much together over the years and they were closer than family.

Ben and Coop talked together alone and made up a poster to announce the sale of the farm. Angie helped Martha clean the kitchen and load their wagon between hugs and tears. Ben would dispatch an ad to Birmingham seeking information on a wagon train heading west by way of the Natchez Trace and the San Antonio Road to Nacogdoches.

Angie's head was swimming. Things were moving so fast now. The trip back that evening was a blur as her imagination ran away with her. She smothered Coop with questions about how, when and what to do for the trip. He calmed her down and said he would make up a list of do's and don'ts for their trek west. He knew there would be friction over his strict possession list that would eliminate so much of their sentimental stuff. He would never forget Ellen's tears and heartache as she packed to move from the city to their humble cabin. She had to leave over half of her fine furnishing at her parents home until their bigger farmhouse was finished. He had his work cut out and wished Ellen was here to advise his daughter and the mood swings to come. The die was cast, he felt alive again. He had Angie and a son in law to be and love would find a way. He hugged his sleepy headed daughter to himself to keep her from falling off the seat. In her dreams she was already in Texas and in the arms of her precious Job.

CHAPTER 24

PROMISED LAND

Big Miller and Job had made good time and arrived on the edge of town before dark. Nacogdoches was a busy place. The cook stove smoke and the camp fires of travelers filled the streets and the smell of pork frying was enticing. The two men dismounted in front of a street vendor frying pork and fry bread. Job wouldn't touch the pork but bought a piece of the fry bread. He kept a jar of honey in his saddle bag to sweeten his coffee so he and Big sat down on a slab bench for supper. They got directions for the post office and the land office from the vendor. The vendor also offered them a place to bed down beside his wagon. They would have hot bread and coffee at their pleasure in the morning. It was nine o'clock that night before the streets calmed down enough for sleep.

The town rose with the sun the next morning. The sounds of chopping wood, livestock being harnessed and peddlers were all around. Job had to relieve himself and did what Pop said to do in these public situations. He obeyed the scripture and turned and pissed on the wall of the shed next door. They enjoyed hot bread and coffee for two bits and rode off in search of the post office. A crowd of men were gathered in front of the building reading the ads for help wanted. There was an obvious shortage of manpower and this made Job feel better. He might get room and board plus the dollar a day for his skills. He could see from the demand that Big and Spike may never leave East Texas. They passed into the post office and gave their names to the clerk for receiving mail. Lo and behold, Big's wife had a letter from her sister and this made their day! They registered to receive future mail and posted their letters back east.

The land office was across the street so they made a bee line for the door. They were the first customers and two clerks grunted as they approached the counter.

Big spoke first, "We'd like information on land grants here in Texas and any advice you got where a smith, cooper or a harness man might make a start." One turned to put together the grant papers and the other cast a doubtful eye at Job and pointed to a poster on front of the counter.

"Can you read?" he asked sarcastically.

The poster stated, "No Indians or slaves may own land in Texas."

"Yeah I can read, pardner, but that don't apply to me. I'm a U.S citizen!" Job looked him dead in the eye and continued, "I want the same papers and no more wise cracks."

The government clerk was not used to such boldness as he knew he had crossed the line. "Yes sir, everything you need right here, applications, descriptions, coordinates and fees to finalize the deed. He passed the papers to Job and got busy elsewhere.

The older clerk had enjoyed the spat between the clerk and Job and with a grin and wink at Job, spoke, "Yes sir, they's a demand for your kind out here. You don't have to leave Nacogdoches to make a living at what you do. There's land to the west and plenty to the south. If you got a backbone and are handy with a gun, there's some good bottomland to claim in no man's land on both sides of the Sabine River between here and Scrappin' Valley. There's a little town of saw millers and cotton growers in Burkeville further south but it's mostly settled." The man offered the advice kindly.

"What's this no-man's land and Scrappin' Valley you talking about?" Job asked.

"Ah it's a neutral strip of bottomland that Mexico and the U.S. kinda kept between their patrols to avoid military incidents. Neither outfit ever ventured into the zone. Every desperado, horse thief or murderer took advantage of the hideout and took over down there. The army patrols have cleaned it a little but no enough to take a family in there. There's creeks, thickets, black bears, timber rattlers and outlaws to contend with down there. A few riders have ventured in to check it out for settlement and they never been seen again. You don't tarry in Scrappin' Valley after dark." He finished his discourse and pointed the area out on a map on the wall.

They thanked the clerk and walked out into the warm spring sunshine. Big Miller had no intent at all in no-man's land but Job had it on his mind. If he could figure the boundary of the badlands, he might could carve out a place on the edge of the wild country. The wild life and big timber would more than sustain a large family. It was worth a look-see but right now they needed to mosey around town and pick up on what was the latest in Texas or the Oregon Territory. A saloon or a blacksmith shop would be the best place to gather information. Job dismissed the saloon because of his Indian looks and the danger it would bring to both to walk in together.

The smith shop was blocked out with business. The smitty and three helpers were all elbows and backbone as they rode up.

The smitty glanced up from shoeing a horse and called out, "A full days wait on shoeing and two days on the cooper."

"We looking for first hand news on what's happening in Texas and the Oregon Territory." Big offered, tipping his hat as a friendly gesture.

"West and south in Texas is wide open. Besides no-mans land, you pretty safe here long as you sport a hog leg like you do. If you up to the journey the Oregon Territory offers the best. Now the rumors out of California are far fetched. They say a seed and a bucket of water is all you need to farm there. The climate is real good they tell me. You'll freeze your butt off in Oregon if the Indians don't scalp you on the way." He quipped glancing at Job as he finished.

"We got a smith in our wagon train back at the Angelina River if you interested in some good help." Big reported to the man, only then did he stop and listen.

"A blacksmith settin' out there on the river?" his look was incredulous.

"That's right, folks on the river are bringing work to him," Big replied.

"You tell him to get in here and I'll pay him three dollars a day till I can see what he can do." The blacksmith wiped his hands on his pants then reached up to shake Big's hand.

"Stanley, Leon Stanley, get him in here and we'll talk." the smitty said.

"Alright Mr. Stanley, we'll be in about three-four days." Big tipped his hat and he and Job rode back out of town toward the Angelina River.

They liked what they heard and both men's minds were racing in anticipation of the future. Spike could get rich in East Texas working his anvil. Big wanted the open sky and his hands in the rich dirt and to Job it didn't matter much what he did if Angie was here beside him.

Big whistled out low riding along and said, "Three dollars a day to start! We may lose Spike and his family right here in Nacogdoches!" Big thought out loud.

"A man could sure get ahead at that rate and can't say I'd blame him." Job replied.

"You're right, I'd jump at that offer with all four feet." Big chuckled as they cleared the town traffic and picked up their pace.

They got back to camp after dark that evening and could hear the kids and smell meat frying a hundred yards away. No one saw them arrive until they walked their mounts into the firelight. The kids and Mrs. Miller smothered Big with hugs and kisses. Job even got a hug in the melee. Everyone was talking at once wanting to hear about Texas and Nacogdoches. The men were famished for meat having only fry bread for two days. They ate and shared what they had learned in town. Spike couldn't believe his ears at what he was offered at the blacksmith shop. His wife was so happy she shouted and ran around the campfire dancing with the children.

Job remembered something his daddy often said, "Good news from a far away land make the bones fat." He would quote from the Good Book. It was a good thing to see and he hoped to rejoice like that some day with Angie at his side.

Two days later the wagon train left for Nacogdoches. They camped maybe ten miles out beside a small branch and the next day Job and Spike rode into town to Leon's shop. The two men hit it off right away and Mr. Stanley introduced himself to Job. Spike wanted to give the job offer a try and Mr. Stanley offered them a place to camp on his farm on the edge of town. He took off work an hour and rode with them to the farm. It was situated next to a running creek and very developed for farming. The smithy's house was very nice and spacious. There were two hundred and forty acres surrounding the house and Mr. Stanley said he was thinking of selling half the farm because his shop was lucrative and all he could handle.

"Well don't advertise it till I talk with Big Miller because you may have two buyers on your hands!" Mr. Stanley agreed and they laughed and talked business on the way back to the shop.

Spike and Job were amazed at the great opportunity that lay before them and hastened to camp with the good news. They had never broken camp any quicker than that day as they moved the wagons through Nacogdoches to make camp on the Stanley property before dark.

Londell Stanley greeted them with tea cakes and coffee and her two teenage boys helped with the livestock. They even had access to a corral on the creek. Soon the fires were going and a celebration was in order. There would be meat, potatoes and flour biscuits tonight. The pent up doubts, exhaustion and trail blues were gone. Life was good and hardworking folks were getting a break.

Job's chest was bursting with pride and joy at helping deliver these pioneers to their dream come true. There was a great prayer of Thanksgiving around the campfire that night. Big Miller concluded the prayer by saying, "Our Joshua, with God's help has brought us to our promised land!" Everyone began to clap but Job could only kick the dirt and smile. He later walked to the creek and gazed at the full moon for an hour. He was not a man of many tears but this day and night was overwhelming. He wiped a tear from his face and thanked the Great Spirit for His help and guidance. He whispered a prayer for Angie and wondered how long he would have to wait to see her again. He returned to camp and rolled up in a blanket beside the fire, his mind on Angie and the terrible distance between them. Job dozed off in a deep rest not knowing that the wheels were in motion to bridge the gap that separated him from his sweetheart. Love had found a way and there would be great surprises for Job in the not too distant future.

CHAPTER 25

QUAKER SCHOONER

The for sale poster at Johnson's Corner was fine and dandy advertising the Cooper farm but word of mouth had taken it to Birmingham and Tuscaloosa. There were six riders and a buggy from B'ham a week later to look at the farm. The gentleman in the buggy never walked past the well and offered Coop five hundred dollars above his asking price to retain the farm from other prospective buyers. Coop had one request in the deal and that was that Ellen's grave would be maintained and maybe someday he could visit. The deal was made and the gentleman rode back to B'ham to make the financial arrangements. Coop and Angie would have almost forty five days to pack and leave. They were desperately searching for a wagon train headed west.

Coop's packing list had frustrated Angie and it was a daily haggle over what could be taken. Coop planned to trade his farm wagon for a Conestoga and another mule to match his but must wait on the proceeds from the sale to arrive. He wanted to keep his list on basic essentials a requirement until he purchased the larger wagon. He would surprise Angie by allowing a few more things at the last minute. He had to stand firm a while longer or she would empty the house!

The potatoes and corn were up and the vegetable garden was an everyday chore. Coop spent these days building a picket fence around Ellen's grave. It seemed to add charm to the already well kept farm. The greatest struggle for Coop was the sentimental value of Ellen's possessions. He would take her fine china but not the fine furniture she loved. The plows, farm tools, anvil, seed kegs and water barrel were essential for survival. He was amazed at how the blankets, work clothes, shoes and food staples were piling up.

Angie's kidnapping and Job's philosophy of "walk lightly but carry a big stick" had convinced Coop to prepare for the worst away from the farm. To go along with his percussion rifle he had ordered two of the new Walker Colt .44's that Job carried. The pistols and hundred rounds of ammo had almost broke the bank but he was content in that he could now protect his family on the trail. Every day or two after the chores were done he set up pickets and chunks of wood for target practice behind the house. He needed to learn to shoot a pistol and also teach Angie. They would stuff cotton wads in their ears and fire six rounds each at each practice. Angie was young and steady handed and Coop considered her deadly with the six shooters. They had a lot of fun but hoped there would never be a man on the smoking end of the barrel.

Two weeks into their waiting Coop got word by the mail carrier that a Quaker joiner was building a prairie schooner like the Conestoga so necessary for pioneer traveling. He decided to ride to B'ham with Angie and check it out. They left early the next day and were directed northeast of town to a splendid farm in the meadow. Besides his own, Coop had never seen such a well constructed and maintained house and property. If the wagon was anything like the farm he would leave satisfied.

Isaiah Brown, his wife and ten children were as impressive as the splendid farm. He greeted Coop and Angie outside his huge barn that included a blacksmith shop, cooper racks and joiner tables with tools. Everyone in the place was multicrafted and busy as bees. There were three of the most handsome and stout looking wagons Coop had ever seen parked to the side and another being put together in the shop.

"Greetings brother and sister, please join us," Mr. Brown stepped to Angie's side of the wagon to help her down.

Introductions were made and a cool bucket of drinking water was drawn for the visitors and hopefully customers.

Coop got right to business. "I'm in the market for a Conestoga type wagon and like what I've heard and see parked out here."

Mr. Brown began his sales pitch and pointed out the features of his lifelong creation.

"This wagon is lighter than the original Conestoga but just as durable and maybe better. It has about the same freight space and two good mules could handle it, though four would be the best. All the wagons are sold except the one we are putting together this week." Coop was so impressed with the Quaker's openness and hospitality and the fact that the wagon would be ready in one week he jumped at the opportunity to purchase the wagon. He had brought every penny he could rake and scrape for earnest money and explained his predicament to Mr. Brown. Mr. Brown was very interested in the contents of what was left in Coop's house, especially Ellen's cherry wood china cabinet. A deal was struck and Coop would return in a week with his wagon and whatever furniture he wanted to barter on the deal. What was so sweet about the deal was Mr. Brown had a grown draft mule for sale and he offered to hold it until Coop returned with the option to buy the mule.

"Look's like we may be in far more than we bargained for Coop." Mr. Brown laughed and said as he pointed to the shop. Four of the boys had gathered around Angie entertaining her with their skills and job duties.

"Believe me she's spoken for, Isaiah." Coop replied chuckling. It was good to see young people laughing and enjoying life.

The excitement was so thick between Angie and her daddy you could almost cut it with a knife. Coop was absolutely fired up and felt alive with purpose and objectivity again. He couldn't help but to see the hand of God working for them since he had made his decision to leave for Texas. He felt such purpose and urgency to deliver his daughter to her future husband in Texas. He was ready to get it done, whatever it took.

The money from the sale of the farm was due in the bank at B'ham any day now. The mail rider would pass the word to come in and sign the papers. So much to do with so little a window of opportunity. Everything was falling into place like clockwork and Coop had every reason to believe it would continue to go smoothly.

The next three days were very emotional for Coop and Angie. They got a reality check as Coop rigged a block and tackle to help load the cherry wood china cabinet. Ellen's chair and sewing chest would be kept if at all possible. Everything else had to go. They would load something, weep a moment and hug one another to regain the courage to finish.

Every piece of furniture or keg down to a straight back chair carried memories. Scratches on the table where Ellen sat were precious to both. The little wooden cradle Coop had fashioned with Ellen's help would be spared. He wanted his grandchildren to have the bed. When they moved Ellen's chair her house slippers were found and Coop lost his composure completely. He cried aloud and held the dainty cloth slippers to his face hoping for a scent of his beloved. Angie had to get him stabilized. She took the slippers and whispered, "Daddy I would like to keep these and give them to our first daughter, Ellen, in Texas." There was a complete transformation as hope and life rushed back into Coop's heart.

"My God yes, we're doing the right things!" Coop replied and the crisis was over.

The mail rider dropped by at noon the next day and handed Coop a notice from the bank in B'ham. The money for the farm would be available in three days, one day after they were to pick up their new wagon. That was just fine for they would be able to harness the mules and familiarize with the larger heavier wagon. They would have to spend several nights so they prepared for the stay.

Coop had canvassed the furniture and tied down everything real good but it was still going slow. He didn't want to loosen or crack the china cabinet but every pothole on the trail seemed bottomless. The road was filled with travelers and they got to tell folks they knew goodbye along the way.

When they pulled into the Brown's yard they were greeted by the whole family. Isaiah had anticipated them spending the night and the accommodations were ready. Neither Coop nor Angie had ever experienced such hospitality and kindness from complete strangers. They felt like royalty as they were made to feel at home.

The home of the Brown's was huge and spacious. The furniture was Quaker style but absolutely charming. Practicality was in their blood and Angie was impressed at the serviceability of the kitchen and pantry. She would sketch Job a plan for her kitchen like this one she thought, smiling at herself as they sat at the large table for refreshments.

The one night layover at the Brown's turned into three as Coop had to secure enough cash and a bank letter for credit until he reached a bank in Texas. He would have one whole day to work with the new mule and harness in a double team. He had a lot to learn but Mr. Brown and his sons were patient and all teachers.

All the attention heaped on Angie and the genuine friendship of the Brown family was exactly what they needed since Ellen's passing and the sale of the farm. She was learning so much from Mrs. Brown in the kitchen. There was a time and place for everything on this farm. The day began with bible reading and prayer, with household chores and livestock tended to as breakfast was prepared. At noon a delicious meal was served and everyone stopped to sit and dine. Supper was taken in early evening followed by storytelling and music.

The bank business and wagon purchase were completed and goodbyes were said. The new mule matched up fine with Coop's and the new wagon was splendid. The cherry wood china cabinet had found a permanent place in the Brown's home and this made Angie very happy. Mrs. Brown gave her a new apron for her new home in Texas. The Quakers were so positive and full of faith in God. The kind farewell was exactly what they needed to prepare for the unknown that lay ahead.

CHAPTER 26

WAGON TRAIN HO

The farm was intact and a welcome sight to them both when they arrived home. A surveyor was camped in the potato shed and would finish the property lines the next day. Angie had time before dark to fix a nice supper and they invited the surveyor, Mr. Moore, to sup with them. Mr. Moore was very informed on local and regional news.

"The big push west is in full swing and I know of three wagon trains pulling out pronto." He related, sopping the last drop of red eye gravy from his plate.

"We need to join a train in a hurry cause this place is sold." Coop replied.

"I know one of the trail bosses personally, Jake Fowler, and I'll put your name in as soon as I get back." Moore promised.

"From B'ham they'll pass thru here, so have the mail rider bring word if we are accepted and we'll be ready." Coop instructed Mr. Moore.

"It's done Mr. Cooper, I'm sure Jake will be glad to sign you up with a cook like Angie." He grinned as he praised her cooking. She was already red faced but so happy to hear laughter on the farm again.

Mr. Moore finished up and left at noon the next day. He had marked Ellen's grave as a cemetery on his field notes and this made Coop glad. He promised to go straight to the trail boss in B'ham to sign them up and send word by the mail carrier.

The next few days went slow on the farm. There was not much to do except to tend to the vegetable garden. The mail rider stopped by for a cool drink of water several times and said the roads were full of west bound travelers.

The fourth day and five days before their deadline to leave the farm, the mail carrier rode up with a grin on his face.

"You folks get packed cause you fixin' to light a shuck!" he said as he dismounted at the well.

"You serious?" Coop asked as he drew up a cool bucket of water for the man.

"Yes sir, Jake Fowler's train is about a day's ride behind me and he said tell you to be ready to roll when they come by. He wants you to tie a couple white rags out on the road so he don't pass you by." The carrier never stopped moving and talking as he got his drink, washed his face and got back on his horse.

"Good luck in Texas!" he called as he rode off toward Tuscaloosa.

Coop and Angie were in shock and silent for several minutes. Coop had immediately focused his eyes out back on Ellen's grave. Angie knew she had to divert his attention and grabbed her daddy's hand and began to sing and dance, "Old Suzanna, don't you cry for me, I'm off to big ol' Texas with my daddy and his mule!"

Coop's countenance brightened up and he hopped and skipped around in a circle for a minute.

"Ok that's enough of that, let's go over everything again and go mark the trail like the man said. That train should be by here around noon tomorrow." Coop said as he grabbed a hammer and nail to tack up a white rag.

Angie tore some strips from an old tablecloth and they walked out to the road to mark their farm. The next few hours were bittersweet as they inspected their cargo for the hundredth time. Neither of them slept an hour that night as they reminisced their lives here on the farm.

The next morning after breakfast Coop went out to Ellen's grave and spent an hour. Angie watched as he walked the potato field with his old hat in his hand. He was either talking to himself or praying and she could see his face was wet from tears. She wanted to go comfort him but knew this was a private time and he needed to settle some things in his spirit. He had to let go of the past and he was at the crossroads. Angie was reminded of the scripture her mother often quoted and opened the family bible to Ecclesiastes to read the passage.

"Ecc. 3: 1-7 T o every thing there is a season, and a time to every purpose under heaven: A time to be born and a time to die; a time to plant and a time to pluck up that which is planted; a time to kill and a time to heal; a time to break down and a time to build up; a time to weep and a time to laugh; a time to mourn and a time to dance; a time to cast away stones and a time to gather stones together; a time to embrace and a time to refrain from embracing; a time to get and a time to lose; a time to keep and a time to cast away; a time to rend and a time to sew; a time to keep silence and a time to speak; a time to love and a time hate; a time of war and a time of peace."

How relevant these holy words were to their circumstances, she thought as Coop walked back to the house.

"Listen honey! I think I hear a team driver a long way out." Coop grabbed a drink of water and headed on foot for the road. She had to almost trot to keep up with his long strides. They stopped at the big road and you could see dust over the tree tops a half a mile away. A rider was approaching at a fast trot and he hailed them by removing his hat and waving it at them.

"Cooper farm, I reckon?" he half yelled as he reined to a stop.

"Yes sir, Ely Cooper and my daughter Angie." Coop introduced themselves to the lone rider.

"They call me Pete." as the man tipped his hat at Angie.

"Jake Fowler's wagon train is a half hour behind me and he says if it's possible, he'd like to camp at your place tonight and enjoy some fresh water." He explained. "That way you can sign up and get acquainted with everyone. Your wagon will make nine in our bunch. You was lucky cause Jake don't sign on more than ten wagons."

Coop was quick to reply, "Sure 'nuf, lead 'em in and we'll get ready for you." Coop said as the rider turned his horse back toward the train.

Coop an Angie rushed back to the farm and began to draw water to make ready for the wagon train. Coop had plenty of seed potatoes left in the shed and brought a bushel to the well for cooking.

"I'm sure glad they decided to rest here." Coop said out loud as he went about preparations.

"Me too daddy, we can familiarize with everything and introduce our selves proper." She agreed.

Thirty minutes later the first wagon turned down their lane and there was more noise and commotion than you could shake a stick at. The team drivers barked at their animals, the clanks and bumps of the wagons and kids talking excitedly permeated the air. There was plenty of room for all the wagons in front of the house and Coop went out to point places to park the wagons.

A tall lanky man on a grey horse was out front barking orders to the team drivers. Most of the women and children were walking a little apart from the wagons to avoid the dust.

The man rode up to Coop while tipping his hat, "Jake Fowler, trail boss!" he half shouted above the noise.

"Take over Pete!" he called to the buckaroo Coop had met earlier.

Jake Fowler dismounted and extended his hand while slapping dust from his clothes with his hat.

Coop shook his hand and replied, "Ely Cooper, Mr. Fowler."

"Glad to meet ya and call me Jake from here on out." he said grinning.

"Come on to the well and have a cool drink of water." Coop offered, leading him to the house.

Coop felt humbled but comfortable in this big man's presence. Jake Fowler stood a good six foot tall and was wiry and bowlegged. His face and hands were brown and leathery looking. The steel blue eyes were bordered by crow's feet from grinning and a life of squinching in the sun and dusty trails. His hat was large brimmed with a stampede strap. The grey shirt and pants were in contrast to the turquoise bandana around his neck. He also sported a Walker Colt .44 in a homemade holster that kept the butt of the pistol comfortably above his waistline. Coop had heard rumors of cowboys out west and believed he was seeing one for the first time.

Angie was drawing and pouring water into every kettle and tub they had not packed on their wagon. She drew up a fresh bucket as the two men approached.

"Jake Fowler, this is my daughter, Angie." Coop introduced her to the trail boss.

Jake never extended his hand but drew his hat to his chest and spoke, "Nice to meet you Mam." He kindly replied.

Angie did a little courtesy and said, "Mister Fowler welcome to our home . . . what was our home, and we are so happy to see you!" she filled the gourd dipper and offered Jake a drink. He thanked her and took a long drink of the sweet, cool water.

"Thank you Mam." He replied and turned to Coop, "Ely, let me get camp set up and we'll talk business." He turned and walked back out front. His horse had never left his side or been tethered. He mounted and began to oversee camp arrangements.

An hour later things had settled down and the livestock were being watered and fed. Pete was calling everyone to an assembly and asked that Coop and Angie be there. When all were present and accounted for, Jake Fowler walked to the middle of the crowd and spoke, "First thang, I want you to meet Ely and Angie Cooper. They'll be number nine in this train and we glad to have 'em." Everyone responded in agreement.

"Let's respect this property and enjoy the well water while we got it. Git some rest cause we pullin' out at first light in the mornin'. Everybody make the Coopers welcome and if you got any gripes or complaints, go talk to the good Lord about 'em cause I got the same gripes." Everyone laughed and began to line up to shake Ely and Angie's hand.

After supper of fried potatoes and salt pork, washed down with hot coffee and tea, Jake Fowler walked up to Coop and Angie to sign them up for his wagon train.

"Coop, Angie, I need to make some things clear before I get your John Henry on this contract." Both nodded and Jake continued.

"They's no drankin' or gamblin' between here and Texas. I need you to write up a will in case something happens to one or both of you. We rotate the wagons in line to give everybody a break from the dust. Excuse the French, but they won't be no bitchin' and gripin'. All differences between folks will be settled by me and two or three other neutral parties. Take your complaints and gripes to the Almighty cause I got the same aches and pains you got."

Jake finished his lecture and waited for Coop and Angie's response. Both nodded in agreement and Coop spoke for them both. "Sounds reasonable to us Jake, we agree to your terms."

Jake nodded and pulled a ledger from a leather pouch.

"I need both your signatures right here and that will wrote up be fore daylight. I require half my money now and the other half when we cross the Sabine River into Texas. I expect to reach Texas before the first of June. If you leave the train between here and Texas, we'll settle up the difference."

Coop and Angie listened and mumbled in agreement as they signed the ledger. Coop pulled a money pouch from his shirt and counted out the fee.

"We got a strong box in the lead wagon for your valuables and I'll receipt 'em." Jake offered noticing the wad of cash Coop was carrying.

"I'll take that offer." Coop said as they finished the signing.

Coop and Jake walked off to deposit the ledger and extra cash in the strong box so Angie walked to the cook fire to get acquainted with the ladies.

The mood was festive around the campfire and the ladies pulled Angie right into the conversation and fun. They were passing a toddler from lap to lap and somehow Angie ended up the final baby tender.

One kind lady got right to the point to quench their curiosity as Angie wrestled with the infant.

"Angie, you folks have kin in Texas?" she inquired.

"Yes Mam, my fiancé went ahead to settle a place for our home." She was surprised at what she heard herself say. It was her first time to make public her personal feelings and plans for her future to strangers. She felt so much better and at peace about leaving the farm after her public announcement.

She continued, "His name is Job and just like Mr. Fowler, he has led a wagon train into Texas. He's probably in Nacogdoches and that's where we're headed." She said smiling and beaming with joy as she thought of Job waiting for her.

Everyone was bedding down as Coop returned and he and Angie fixed their pallets outside like everyone else.

"I'm gonna dispatch a letter to forward our mail from Ben Johnson's to Nacogdoches, Texas and forward a letter to Job letting him know we are on the trail west also." Coop informed Angie as they said their good nights.

Pressing Job's letters to her heart she fell asleep knowing that she was only a couple months from Job and their new life in Texas.

CHAPTER 27

NO MAN'S LAND!

Every working man that had rode into Texas with Job was working a job in or around Nacogdoches. Spike had signed on at Leon's blacksmith and Big Miller was to sharecrop Mr. Stanley's cleared fields for the rest of the summer and then winter in Nacogdoches. Mr. Stanley gave permission to build cabins so the pioneers set to work on their futures.

Mr. Stanley had pulled some strings with the town council for permission to let Mrs. Wells teach the three R's to any child within walking distance of the farm.

Mr. Stanley learned of Job's skill with leather and harness and referred all repairs and new harness to him. He would repair or supply the rings and latches that Job needed. The demand on Job was great but he had the liberty to come and go as he pleased, working for himself. He still had no-man's land and the river bottom on his mind. He had asked the locals and gathered all the information he could about the territory and was planning a week's trip down river. Big Miller was very knowledgeable of farm and wagon harness and was working with Job along with tending the fields. In a couple of days, the two men had caught up on leather repairs so Job decided to take his trip down river. Big was concerned about him traveling alone into outlaw country but no one could afford to leave their jobs and Job would not put them at risk venturing into the wilderness.

Job wrote a will with Angie being his heir. He deposited all his cash in the bank except for ten dollars in silver and left the will with Big.

He was very excited about his trip and even Red, the mule, seemed to sense the new adventure. Job had carefully packed his weapons and ammunition. The chewing tobacco and the rock candy were essentials to both him and the mule.

Job's plan was to ride southeast and skirt the road back east to Milam then explore the territory south as far as Burkeville. He learned that there were a few settlers scattered among the hills and along the creeks that might have knowledge of the area.

After breakfast and the bible reading on Sunday morning, Job rode out on his scouting trip. His plan was to ride hard until he cleared the settlements then slow down and be more cautious. The area he was riding into was known for bushwhackers.

Job had left civilization by dark and happened upon a small farm clearing at dusk. He let out a piercing yell to let the folks know of his presence then waited for an answer. A few minutes later a call came back from beside the log cabin so Job rode into the yard. A long Tom barrel was following his every move from the corner of the house. He never dismounted but sat waiting. A man's voice came from the shadows beside the cabin.

"What's yer business here, Mister?" the voice barked.

"Ridin' south to Burkeville. 'Preciate any hep on the trail ahead," Job replied with as kind a voice as he could muster.

"You probably three days ride from town, the trail's plain with chopped marks. Move on outta here, cause I don't know ya." The man ordered in a serious tone.

"Thanks, Mister." Job answered and reined Red down the trail south. Job could sense the suspicion and fear in the farmer's voice so he decided it was time to pay more attention to his surroundings on the trail ahead. Finding a little clearing off the trail, he kicked around in the dark to drive away any mice or snakes then fixed a pallet for the night. He tied Red close then laid down with his pistol under the blanket on his chest. He would risk a fire after daylight but not at night in this country. He fell asleep wondering what Pop was doing on the Big Pond in Savannah.

He was awake long before daylight and when his eyes adjusted to the dimness, he got up and gathered wood for a fire. He broke out his coffee can and was sipping fresh coffee and nibbling on a cat head biscuit Mrs. Miller had packed for his trip. Red was fidgeting and snortin' wanting his hand full of corn to start the day.

Job was on the trail again thirty minutes later. He would ride a mile or so then stop and listen. The trail south was dim and a chop mark was made on a large tree every quarter mile or so. The trail followed the clearings and skirted the steep hills and hollows. The creeks and springs were plentiful so this is where Job would search for signs of other travelers or bushwhackers. The outlaws were no accounts that refused to work and preyed on decent folks. Pop had called them scallywags and always used a verse from the bible to describe them.

"He that tilleth his land shall be satisfied with bread; but he that followeth vain persons is void of understanding." Proverbs 12:11

The no accounts had nothing to do but lay around and devise ways and means to get something for nothing. Vigilante justice was the rule of law in these parts and if you had trouble, it would be bad. To steal a horse or violate a white woman called for a hanging or killing. The outlaws knew this and if they trespassed, they would leave no witnesses.

The trail had been a little rough but Job had kept his bearing and approached the town of Burkeville, Texas in the afternoon of the third day. He had skirted a few cotton fields and near town, a peck mill was sawing rough lumber. A dry goods store, small church and a barrel house for tobacco and potatoes made up the town that straddled the wagon trail headed east to the Sabine River and west on the cattle trails. Lumber was stacked everywhere and the stench from animal hides stretching and curing filled the air.

The local mercantile store served as a post office, courtroom, employment office and any other local business along with news and views. Job walked his mule to a hitch post and carefully surveyed the locals lounging around on the front porch. His approach had grown a few stares and nudging among the customers. He dismounted half hitched his mule to the post and began stomping the stiffness from his legs. He kept his hand on the pistol and never turned his back to the crowd. A scrawny lad about ten years old approached him with a bucket in hand and a proposition,

"Water dat mule fer five cents mister?" he asked.

"Yep, much obliged," Job answered, seeing there was no water trough available close by. The lad ran for the water as Job made his way to the front door.

A large unkept and mean looking fellow was leaning against the stoop post and remarked, "Yore kind uses the back door, Mister!" he emphasized "back door" as malice flickered in his eyes.

Every town has its local loud mouthed know it all, so Job figured this fellow was maintaining his reputation. Job never acknowledged the man's presence or responded to his remark, but stopped, reached down and unsheathed his pig sticker from his boot top, repositioned it and continued into the front door of the store. The bully could be heard cussing and garnering support from the other idlers.

The store keep met Job in the front of the slab counter, brandishing a hickory axe handle.

"Back door, Mister, Injuns and blacks, go to the back door." he directed emphatically.

Job stopped two strides into the room and responded, "You want my silver, you serve me out front!"

"Can't do that, it'll ruin my business, now get out a here!" the clerk ordered.

This was his first real dose of public discrimination and it set his blood to boiling but Job knew he was outnumbered and not welcome in this town. He took the two steps backward to the door and eased back to the mule.

The water boy had returned with a bucket of water but the loud mouthed fellow had kept him from watering Red. Job unhitched the mule and mounted, at the same time drawing his pistol and laying it across his lap.

"Your mouth is about to overload your ass, Mister." Job said coldly, staring down the bully. The large man was surprised at Job's good English and swallowed hard not able to reply.

Job reined the mule back the way he came out of town and headed back northwest to Nacogdoches. Others had made his decision for him about settling anywhere near the Sabine River. He knew better than to heap all the folks into one basket and resent everyone. The problem was, the good people never spoke out or stood for what was right until it was too late. Though the sun was shining and spring was pushing through, there was a dark cloud over Job's thoughts. His closest relative was a thousand miles away, his hopes and plans for the future seemed to have been extinguished by the racists behind him. What was it that his daddy had told him?

"Son, the world is a big place, don't get yourself boxed in by little people and never give up hope!" Job's eyes filled with tears. He readjusted his hat, took a long look at the blue sky, suddenly heard the red birds singing and decided right then and there that the mully grubs was for hopeless people.

Angie was waiting his beckon call, Pop had grubstaked him and he had real friends in Nacogdoches. He camped early that night and roasted a swamp rabbit for supper. He half grinned at his new awakening and the last thought he had before bedding down that night was, I need to get on with living and leave the dead alone! A red wolf howling in the river bottom soothed his troubled spirit and he fell into a much needed sleep that night.

CHAPTER 28

NO PLACE LIKE HOME

Leon Stanley's farm was a sight for sore eyes as Job rode into Big Miller's camp that Sunday afternoon. Big was notching poles for a corn crib and was all a big grin as Job dismounted.

"Well look what the dog's drug up!" Big exclaimed, giving Job a vigorous handshake.

"It's good to see you, Big. I ain't heard nothing but my own fart in three days!" Job remarked, casting an appreciative eye on the corn crib and the new temporary cabin under construction.

The children were swarming all around Job as he unsaddled Red and began to rub him down while checking for cuts and bruises.

The children's minds had not been poisoned by prejudice and bigotry so Job loved every minute of their attention.

Mrs. Miller had seen Job ride in and was preparing leftovers and a fresh pot of coffee. Everyone gathered beneath a red oak tree as Mrs. Miller served the food and coffee.

The children were expecting a story of Job's adventure so he obliged them as he wolfed down the vittles. He never even hinted about the bad reception he got down river.

After the meal, Big and Job took a walk and Job shared the details of his scouting trip through Scrappin' Valley and into Burkeville.

"I seen some fine bottomland downriver, Big. I never met anybody or had no trouble but you could hide an army in those hills and hollers." Job said, describing the wilderness he had scouted.

"Did you make it to Burkeville?" Big asked.

"Yeah, I sure did but I wadn't there five minutes, back door service for people of color. They was a loud mouth stirring up things so I skedaddled!" Job reported the incident in a cool tone.

"Wadn't another two dollar shootout was it?" Big asked, slapping Job on the back, hoping to lighten up the moment.

"No, I wanted to put my foot in the feller's mouth. I'll ride back down there someday and check things out." Job declared.

"They's one bad apple in every dozen, maybe next time you'll meet the good folks," Big encouraged his friend. "In the meantime, there's plenty to do around here. Me and Spike's got a deal for you if you're interested," Big paused to watch the sunset through the treetops.

"I'm listening." Job answered back.

"We got two cabins and fence to build before winter. Spike will have to work at the smith's every day but Sunday. Me and you could trade off between harness repairs and carpenter work. Spike is offering to pay you a fair day's wage to work on his place. 'Course if you get ants in your britches again, we'll let you go for a while," Big finished with a chuckle.

"I appreciate the offer and accept. Ya'll just show me what ya'll want done!" Job's spirit had immediately lifted realizing he was accepted and his services needed by such good people. He was reminded of a saying from the Good Book his daddy often quoted, "Without a vision, the people will perish."

He felt right at home with these pioneer folk and planned to keep up his end of the deal.

Big and Spike had drew up plans for their cabins and out buildings. Job got together with them and talked over the details. He wanted to get them prepared for winter but he was also making plans for a nice shelter for his future bride. The Stanley farm was almost occupied and he wanted elbow room on his place.

The Stanley farm was like a beehive of activity for the month of April. Job was a craftsman with an axe, adze and a crosscut saw. The women and children were chinking the cracks in the walls with clay and moss as the walls went up. Each cabin had a large mud chimney and Spike was forging the pot hangers and spits at work. The women folk would keep a plate of teacakes and coffee at Job's worksite and a crude sketch of a bench or table would often be conveniently placed for him to see!

The three R's, readin', ritin' and 'rithmatic were being taught three days a week by Mrs. Wills and a dozen children were in attendance. Mrs. Wills was constantly picking Job for more information on herbs and home remedies to complete her farmer's almanac.

She had enlisted Job's service on several occasions to accompany the children on field trips to learn all they could about local plants and their uses.

The spring rains had slacked off some and Job was splitting shakes for the cabin roofs and doing leather repairs a couple a days a week. He wound up being a babysitter at the local swimming hole on Saturdays which lead to making a lot of new friends around town. The locals seemed so surprised that an Indian could read, write and even do numbers! The children accepted him at face value and that was his goal, to educate and influence a generation to resist and reject racial segregation and prejudice. He still met resistance and hostility but it was isolated. The European immigrants were the new targets of hostility since the Indian population was pushed to the north into Oklahoma. The Europeans were subtly pushed south and southwest to settle the more arid regions of Texas.

Payday on Saturday and the approach of a mail carrier were the most exciting times each week. When a mail carrier arrived in town, the news spread like wildfire. A member or two of each family would hurry to the post office to check the mail for news from back east. There would be cries of joy, tears and shouts of gladness all over town at mail call.

Big Miller was in Nacogdoches at the land office when word of the mail carrier's arrival was received. He loafed along with the crowd and stood waiting as the postal clerk called names as he emptied the pouch.

"Irvin, Job Irvin!" the clerk shouted across the crowd. Big responded with a loud "Hey!" and pushed through the crowd to retrieve Job's mail. The clerk knew Big and Job as close friends then handed him several letters. Big couldn't help but glance at the addresses on the letters and he couldn't hold back a laugh out loud.

"Boy, this jest makes my day!" He grinned all over as he read the name of Angie Cooper in the corner of the letters.

Big Miller's camp was like an ant hill of activity when he arrived after dinner. A hobo supper had been called for Saturday evening and a huge kettle of venison was on the fire. Each family that came to the supper would bring a vegetable or spice to add to the kettle of meat. Fried cornbread and cat head biscuits were in abundance and always several huckleberry cobblers or possum grape jelly was for dessert.

Job and Spike were setting up tables and benches beneath the red oak shade trees. Spike began picking at Big for loafing off to town when there was so much work to be done. Big just smiled and walked to the cook fire where he greeted his wife with a kiss on the cheek. Job couldn't help but notice that Big drew her close and whispered in her ear. Mrs. Miller smiled real big and glanced Job's way all big eyed, face beaming. As Big grinned at Job, he got this warm excited feeling all over.

"What is it Big?" Job asked grinning back.

Big patted his shirt and began to unbutton it where he slowly pulled out several envelopes.

Job's mouth fell open and he asked, "For me?"

Big just grinned real big and extended the letters to Job. A letter from back east excited everyone and the focus was on Job as with trembling hands and tear filled eyes, he held the envelopes. He scanned the return addresses and there were two letters from Angie and one from Coop!

The silence was broken by Mrs. Miller's sniffles. Job realized there were tears of joy for him all around the campfire. Suddenly, Big Miller grabbed a bucket and said, "Job, why don't you fetch some water?" Job took the cue and headed for the spring for a few minutes alone.

Finding his favorite spot beside a huge cypress knee, Job sat down and held the letters to his face, longing for the scent of his sweetheart. After a while, he noticed the postmarks and realized two were from the Cooper farm and the third from Angie was from Jackson, Mississippi!

He swiftly read through each letter and started over trying to process all the information. His heart ached for both Angie and Coop at the loss of Ellen and their decision to sell the farm and follow him to Texas.

Jackson, Mississippi! Why Angie could only be weeks away from Nacogdoches. He wanted to pack Red and ride east to meet the wagon train but knew that would be foolish. He needed to get a place ready for Coop and Angie before winter!

Job arrived back at the campfire and hugged everyone's neck. He read the letters out loud to everyone, except for the mushy stuff from Angie. New people would be arriving! News from back home, loved ones coming west! This is just what the hobo supper needed to liven up everything!

Before the hobo shindig was over, Job spoke to Big and Spike about a shelter for Angie and Coop. They all three approached Leon Stanley and he gladly offered a place to erect another cabin. A seasoned farmer like Coop would be a great asset to the community. Job was really touched when everyone came by to offer their help to finish a cabin for them.

As Job made ready for bed that night, a word from the Good Book that his mother often quoted, came to him, "As cold waters to a thirsty soul, so is good news from a far country." Proverbs 25:25 Wiping salty tears from his face, Job whispered a Thank You! to the Great Spirit and spoke into the darkness, "There's no place like home!"

CHAPTER 29

U.S CALVARY

Jake Fowler's wagon train had made good time the last six weeks. They had averaged 15-20 miles a day and sometimes a little more if no one busted a wheel or harness. Jake was a no nonsense man and was known on the trail west. He never looked for trouble and trouble avoided him. His reputation preceded him and that served everyone well. Pioneers traveling west needed dry goods and they spent money. The local markets and farms along the way prospered from the pioneers. The hawkers and snake oil peddlers tended to avoid Jake Fowler's outfit and this suited him just fine.

Angie and Coop had found their place among the group of the pioneers. The daily grind and dusty travel was tempered by all the friendships being forged. Coop had related the incident of Angie's kidnapping and she was somewhat of a celebrity in the minds of a lot of folks. The part of a Cherokee Indian rescuing her was retold occasionally at suppertime around the fires. Angie dared not reveal her relationship with Job to the other travelers. A lot of folks would frown on a white woman in the company of an Indian, even one half white, decent and educated. Both whites and Indians were suspicious of a half breed.

The wagon train was approaching a popular camp site on the Natchez Trace called White Oak and the decision made to camp there for the night. A squad of U.S. Calvary was also camped there so Jake Fowler made their acquaintance while the wagon train broke out of harness.

The Calvary troop was invited to eat supper in Jake's camp and the arrangements were made. The officer in charge, Joshua Robert Brown, would dine with the civilians in their camp and the troopers would fill their plates and cups and eat back at their bivouac. Fraternizing was strictly forbidden by Army regulations. The troopers were very happy to get a "home cooked meal" as they called it. The ladies put out a little more effort that evening to show their appreciation for the troopers. These men kept the roads west open and protected them from Indians and outlaws.

After supper, Jake Fowler took the opportunity to glean information on the trail ahead.

"Lieutenant Brown, what does the trail look like between here and Natchez?" Jake enquired.

"It's pretty good travelin' 'tween here and the Mississippi. Word of mouth is the road is clear all the way to Texas." Lieutenant Brown responded.

"Any new trespass levies or scalawags we need to prepare for?" Jake continued.

"Same old hardheads and not too much trouble at the levy crossings since the shootout at the big cut a few months back." The Lieutenant said matter of factly.

"A shootout, anybody kilt?" Jake asked.

"One of the Clopp boys out of Natchez almost lost a leg. He says an Injun ambushed him and tried to scalp him. I know better. Word on the trail was they tried to charge five dollars a wagon to pass over the big cut and a half breed trail boss headin' up a Carolina wagon train, disagreed!" the Lieutenant chuckled relating the incident.

Coop and Angie could hardly believe what they were hearing. The description of the trail boss and being several months passed, fit Job perfectly.

Coop could not contain himself any longer and spoke, "Lieutenant, Jake, I believe that Injun trail boss you speakin' of is the feller that rescued my daughter, Angie!" he finished with a smile at Angie.

"Well, we need men like that out here, even if he is a breed!" Jake interjected with emotion in his voice.

"Miss Angie, let's have a readin' from the Good Book before we turn in." Jake continued and Angie went for the bible in her wagon.

Angie was a superb reader. She had chosen the story of the Hebrews exodus from Egypt, for she said, "It related to their situation very well."

Late that night, Angie lay awake listening to the night sounds. The snores, farts, animals stomping and the whine of mosquitoes could not dampen the joy of what she heard that night. Somewhere, not far away, her beloved was probably gazing at the same stars she saw through the tree branches overhead.

The story of the Hebrews exodus from Egypt and Jehovah's care and provision for them in the wilderness was so related to their situation. Just in the nick of time, God would come through for them. Tidbits of information, like the Lieutenant's story tonight, Ellen's gravesite preserved, the farm selling so quickly, the new wagon purchased from the wonderful Quaker family, all enforced her belief that they were part of a divine plan. She wiped away tears as she thought of her Mother and a saying she often quoted, "God works in mysterious ways His wonders to perform."

Perfect peace filled her heart and she thanked God for His divine care.

CHAPTER 30

A HELPING HAND

Leon Stanley's farm was a beehive of activity with all the construction going on and the new school being located there. Job had picked out a cluster of red oak trees for a spot to build his cabin. He wanted shade from the hot noon and evening sun. The neighbors all pitched in to get the heavy walls up and the roof on, rain tight. He would work on the mud chimney and furniture in late summer. The leather repair business had slowed down a bit so he and Big Miller were able to focus on the carpenter and joiner work that was necessary. The ladies kept a drawing or design for furniture in front of them at all times. Big Miller took the opportunity to bribe the ladies for teacakes and other sweets to be available also. His philosophy was, "A man will think clearer and work harder if his belly is full!" The message got across to the ladies for there was always a plate of something sweet beneath the tablecloth where they worked.

One day at noon, the local magistrate rode up to Big's camp and introduced himself to Big and Job. David Jacks was a big man with a friendly disposition. He stood for law and order and most everyone liked him.

He shook hands and spoke, "Big, Job, we got a problem at the town hall and was hoping you could help us." he cut to his reason for stopping by.

"Sure thang." Big nodded, "What's going on?" he asked.

"We got some field notes, deeds and other official papers that's needed down in Burkeville pronto. The trip back to Gaines Ferry and down river will take too long. Job here is one of the few men that's made the trip through Scrappin' Valley and back to live to tell it. We was hopin' you could ride back down there on official business. It will pay a man ten dollars!" David Jacks emphasized the good pay.

Big and Job eyeballed each other and both were just looking for a chance to get away from being hen pecked.

Job discreetly nodded his consent to Big and replied, "I could use the cash sheriff, plus these women are working my hands raw on all this furniture!" Job responded holding his palms out to show the blisters. They all laughed and Big agreed that they would both go and split the wages. They would ride into Nacogdoches the next morning and pick up the mail pouch for Burkeville. David Jacks was pleased and after a half dozen teacakes and coffee, he rode back to town with the good news.

"This says a lot for you and our families, Job. No longer than we've been here and folks are trusting us with such an important task," Big said with pride and satisfaction.

"A good name is rather to be chosen than great riches." Job quoted from the Good Book. This habit of quoting from ancient proverbs and wise sayings came from his daddy, Tad, and Pop.

Both men began to put away their tools to get ready for the trip the next day. Big strolled off to tell his wife, while Job packed his gear and checked Red, the mule, for cuts and bruises in his feet. He roped Big's mount and inspected the mare the same way. In his excitement and anticipation for the new adventure, he had begun whistling a tune his daddy, Tad, had taught him so long ago.

Big Miller and Job were at the land office at the crack of dawn the next morning. The mail pouch was of considerable size so Job tied it behind his old saddle on Red. Their plans were to be gone no longer than a week. The sheriff sent a note along with them giving them the authority to protect the mail pouch.

Job took the lead and they traveled at a good clip for two hours. A small creek supplied a cool drink for the animals. Job snacked on blackberries and dug a few wild onions while giving the animals a breather. He offered Big a handful of the delicious berries.

"Unh, unh, no thank ye! They'll go straight through me!" Big grinned, refusing the offer.

"Everyone needs a good purgin' once in a while." Job advised.

Mounting up, they rode another two hours before stopping for dinner. Mrs. Miller had packed a poke of biscuits and a jar of molasses. Red whined for his piece of rock candy and Job obliged. Grass was plentiful in the open spots but Job observed the mule reaching overhead to nibble on the tender oak branches.

Job broke the silence and said, "Big, you got any ideas why a mule or donkey will mix a bite of oak leaves with his grass?"

"Nope, maybe it's a spice to him," Big replied shaking his head.

"That's what I figure, they are a little tangy cause I tried 'em." Job said, mounting his mule.

"An oak eatin' Injun, try saying that three times real fast!" Big remarked and laughed out loud.

The men had decided to ride from can to can't or dark thirty, as the locals call it. Big had brought along a splinter hatchet so they could add more chop marks or blazes on the larger trees to aid other riders traveling southeast. If they figured it right, the government would move more mail on this route if Job and Big delivered it in a record time. Three weeks wages for one week on horseback was "high cotton," as Big put it. They might have to sleep without a fire or roast a rabbit in daylight but it was well worth the trouble.

By the third day of hard riding, they were about two hours from Burkeville and were following an open trail wide enough for a wagon. A pole bridge had been laid across a steep banked creek and right smack dab in the middle of the bridge, a wagon sat having a wheel that fell between the poles up to the hub.

A young man was using blocks and a long pole in an attempt to lift the wagon high enough to move it. The cargo of potatoes, squash and other sundries had been unloaded. A young woman was riding the pole like a stick horse trying to help her husband free the wagon. Three children were standing to the side, watching. As soon as the man saw Big and Job, he stopped working, reached inside the wagon, pulled out a scatter gun and waited for their approach.

Big waved a hand and shouted "Hello!" in a friendly gesture. Stopping their mounts at the creek bank, Big introduced themselves, "Howdy folks, I'm Big Miller and this here is Job Irvin out of Nacogdoches, we ridin' into Burkeville on official business for the magistrate."

Job pulled out the letter from sheriff Jacks and offered it to the man.

"Howdy!" the man replied, crossing the bridge and taking the note from Job. Scanning the letter he lowered his weapon and continued, "J.L. Rackley, wife Leann and our chillin', Greyson, Alaina and Landon," he proudly pointed to each family member as they shyly nodded at the two strangers.

"How 'bout us lending a hand," Job offered cautiously as he dismounted.

"Yes sir, ya'll get down and have a look!" Mr. Rackley offered.

Leann left the bridge and joined the children on the creek bank. The men approached the wagon and immediately Big offered to make an adjustment to the jack rig. While J.L. took lead on the draft horses, Job shoved and lifted from behind. In two huffing and puffing shoves, the wagon eased out of the drop off. Mr. Rackley was all grin and his family was clapping and cheering on the creek bank.

"I shore'preciate the hep," J.L. said as he removed his hat and extended his hand in a Thank You!

After a careful inspection of the wagon wheel and hub, the wagon was reloaded. Big and Job asked to ride along with the Rackley's into town.

As they rode along, both parties shared bits and pieces of news locally and from back east. Every issue of the day was discussed and before they knew it, they approached the town. Mr. Rackley reined in his wagon and apologetically spoke to Job.

"Mr. Irvin, I can't hep but notice you got to be part Injun or Mexkin. As far me, that's fine and dandy! But in this town, they's a few instigators or loud mouths, if you please. Be shore and watch yore back," he advised in a dead serious tone.

"Thanks J.L., I thank I met that jackass down here before. I jest don't want to drag your family into my troubles." Job responded in kindness.

"Well I'm hungry and thirsty, let's hold this serious stuff for later," Big barked with a grin and a slap of his hat on his leg. He took the lead into town and headed for the mercantile store where most of the local business took place.

The Rackley's were well known locally and several people waved or spoke as they rolled past. The party stopped in front of the dry goods store and everyone got down to stretch and freshen up a bit. Just like before, a lad with a bucket approached and offered to water the livestock for five cents a head. The lad was a little shy of Job and he broke the ice by saying, "Git the water boy, this time you'll git paid!" and grinned at the lad. The boy grinned back real big and lit out to fetch a bucket of water. Big, glanced at Job with a puzzled expression at his remark to the water boy. Job added to his curiosity by saying, "You'll see soon enough!"

CHAPTER 31

NACOGDOCHES

The "mighty" Mississippi was an understatement to the folks on Jake Fowler's wagon train. The river ferry crossing at Natchez was exciting to the travelers. Most had never seen such a large river and bristling economy. The crossing took up most of the day so the pioneers had time to restock their supplies. The prices for essentials would more than triple the further west they moved.

Angie and Coop were careful to listen for any information on Job's wagon train. The ferry master at Natchez remembered an "Injun trail boss" and gave them some words of caution about not trespassing on the plantations and on protecting their livestock.

The late spring rains made the trail west from Natchez to Nacogdoches very difficult for animals and humans. Most folks would rather walk than ride the rough wagons. Everyone had fashioned a walking stick to keep from slipping down in the gumbo mud. The mud clung to your feet like snow shoes and if anyone fell down, they had to have help getting up. The one thing that kept everyone's spirits up was the fact that Texas was almost in sight.

The river crossing at Alexandria was a little tricky because of high water. Jake Fowler never took chances with people's lives. He laid over two days until the water dropped to safely cross. He then used a mule team and ropes to guide each wagon across.

The wagon trains arrival at Gaines Ferry on the Sabine River turned into a festival atmosphere! The ladies were crying and laughing openly and tears could be seen making tracks on the men's faces.

Angie remembered from the bible, how the Hebrew women celebrated the crossing of the Red Sea from Egypt. Miriam had played a tambourine, sang and danced in praise to Jehovah for His care. She pulled out a skillet and a spoon and began to parade around in celebration. Before it was over, hats were flying and even the mules were braying at the excitement. The wagon train made camp in Texas that night and folks sat up late talking and rejoicing over their future.

The mail riders had been reliable by bringing news out of Texas and enjoyed a minute or two of gossip over a homemade biscuit or teacake. The reports from Nacogdoches were promising and Jake Fowler had no trouble with stragglers. Everyone was anxious to see the new territory and possibly meet up with friends and relatives. Angie and Coop expected Job to pop up along the trail anytime!

Jake Fowler's wagon train made quite a stir arriving in Nacogdoches. It was Saturday afternoon and the town was hopping with activity. It was payday for the saw mill and field laborers. The smell of fried pork chitlins and bread filled the air. The first place a traveler or wagon would stop was the blacksmith shop at the edge of town. There was room for wagons to park and livestock hobbled or corralled. Jake Fowler and Pete swung into action by positioning the wagons and livestock.

The blacksmith, Leon Stanley, walked out to meet Jake and the newcomers. Spike continued working in the shop and wondered if there would be any news or anyone kin to his neighbors.

Jake left Pete to setting up the camp and rode over to Leon.

"Boy, you're a sight for sore eyes!" Jake said grinning and slapping the dust from his clothes.

The men shook hands and Leon replied, "Same here, Jake. That's a mighty fine outfit you brought out this time," he remarked as he admired the well kept wagons and the people busy with their chores.

"Good God fearing folks, Leon. Drop by in an hour or so for coffee and I'll introduce you." Jake offered.

Leon did not tarry for he had made arrangements years ago to accommodate Jake Fowler's wagons. Jake was a man of few words but a lot of action. He had walked to the center of the camp and called for a meeting in an hour.

Angie and Coop were busy sorting out things for the night and anxious to ask around town about Job. The ladies were busy planning the supper meal and Angie joined them, hoping to work off some of her nervous energy. A wood cutter had conveniently arrived and Coop walked over to help purchase firewood.

Everyone was talking at once and Coop finally got to ask the woodcutter if he had heard of Job Irvin.

"They's a young feller works for Leon Stanley, name of Job," the man replied. Coop was ecstatic and couldn't wait to tell Angie.

Everything had settled down a bit and folks had gathered at the campfire for the meeting with Mr. Fowler.

Almost to the minute, Jake walked up with Leon Stanley for the business meeting. Coffee was served and Jake got to the point immediately.

"First of all I want to thank the Lord for one of the best trips and group of people that I've ever rode with!" Jake looked around at the crowd and said smiling, "I wish I could turn you around and take you back!" Everyone burst out laughing.

"Anyhow," he continued, "We made it safe and sound. I want everyone to know we are guests here on Leon Stanley's property. Just conduct yourselves like you have all along and things will be fine. After breakfast and bible readin' in the morning, we'll settle up and you'll be on your own. I'll send word for the sheriff to meet with us for breakfast to catch up on the news here bouts. Jest remember this ain't Atlanta or B'ham! Pay attention to what's goin' on and don't take no wooden nickels!" Jake finished up and turned to get his cup of coffee. Folks began to make ready for night and a few men walked into town to check things out.

Coop had not told Angie what the woodcutter said about Job so while she worked in the wagon, he caught up with Leon Stanley and introduced himself.

"Ely Cooper, from Alabama," Coop said as he shook Leon's hand.

"How can I hep you?" Leon asked smiling.

"I've got kin folk somewhere out here, Job Irvin by name and the woodcutter said he might work for you." Coop stated his situation.

"Most certainly do, fine young fellow! Next to Jake Fowler, he's the best trail boss we seen out here. He does leather repair for me and other folks when he can. Right now he's out of town on a mail run down south to Burkeville." Leon stated.

"Any idea when he'll get back?" Coop asked.

"Can't say, probably a seven or eight day trip barring he don't have trouble. Him and another feller, Big Miller, rode out together. I think they been gone a week now." Leon stated all he knew of Job's whereabouts.

"By the way, Job's working on a cabin out at my place when he's not gallivanting' off. The folks he brought out on the trail are spending the winter out there. Spike, my partner there, he's a buddy of Job." Leon remarked and pointed at Spike shoeing a horse in the shop.

"Come on over, I'll introduce you," Leon offered kindly.

New arrivals were always welcome and exciting but when Spike met Ely Cooper and learned of Angie's arrival he was very happy. The men agreed to meet the next day and Spike would lead the Cooper's out to the Stanley farm.

Sunday morning was like a holiday for the new arrivals to Nacogdoches. At daybreak, the cook fires were ablaze and the smell of coffee and biscuits filled the cool morning air. Folks were anxious and ready to get on with their new lives. Some would winter in or around Nacogdoches and others would move further west.

After breakfast and Bible reading, Jake Fowler introduced the sheriff, David Jacks, and he informed the people about local services and laws. Jake was pleased the sheriff was present as he opened the safe and settled accounts. The safe contained some jewelry and several thousand dollars in cash and coins. Him and Pete had kept a watchful eye on any strangers hanging around and they were always armed.

That afternoon, Spike rode into camp, and after all the goodbye's, Coop and Angie hitched their wagon and followed Spike out of town to the Stanley farm. In less than an hour, they sat admiring the new cabin Job was building for them. Everyone was still in their Sunday's best and welcomed the new family.

Coop and Angie refused the invitation to share a cabin and chose to stay with their wagon in the fair weather. Job's cabin would afford shelter from the wind and rain but Angie wanted him present for the special occasion to move in.

Angie had one important thing to do before dark. Coop helped her get access to the clothes trunk where she pulled out the pinafore Job had given her so long ago. Angie lay the pinafore beside her pallet in the wagon. After bedding down, she pulled the pinafore to her face to wipe the hot tears of joy that she had been holding back all day. She wished her Mother could be here to share the moment. She remembered a rhyme Ellen shared with her and she whispered it into the cool night air, "Love will find a way and tough love will get you through each day!"

CHAPTER 32

BIG CLEANS A PLOW!

Job politely opened the door to the store and waved the Rackley's in first then he followed Big into the building.

The store keep, Andrew Burks, greeted everyone then cast a cool eye at Job.

"Me and you done crossed this bridge before, hadn't we feller?" Mr. Burks remarked to Job. A tense silence followed with everyone puzzled not knowing of Job's visit before.

"It's not a bridge, it's an opinion!" Job replied icily. "All I need from you is to tell me where the town hall or the sheriff can be found."

Mr. Burks was speechless for a moment then replied, "Two buildings down on the right, Cooter Griggs is sheriff and the town's business is done there."

"I'll be outside!" Job glanced at Big and left the store.

The mood in the room was quiet and tense till Big spoke, "Mister, we here on official business for the sheriff out of Nacogdoches. Now I don't know what's going 'tween you and my partner but I'm getting to dislike you real quick!" Big was red faced and itchin' to get ahold of the store keep.

"The signs on the door, colored people and Injuns use the back door or side window!" Mr. Burks replied nervously.

"Is that your policy or politics?" Big asked, putting the man on the spot.

"Sir, it's not my opinion but that's the way it's always been here. If I let a man of color in my front door, it could ruin my business." Mr. Burks explained his position.

No one expected what came next, but Leann Rackley spoke, "Its local politics Big, and you know it Mr. Burks! There's not a half dozen people that agree with that sign on your door. You are afraid of Sid Herd and his bunch. Well, I'm ready for a change and if that sign don't come down, we'll start buying dry goods by the barrel off the river!" Leann was red faced and shaking her finger at Mr. Burks when she finished.

A small crowd had gathered since their arrival. Most everyone was grunting or nodding their head in approval of what Leann had said. J.L. couldn't be silent any longer and he did as much business in town as anyone. His grandfather had been a pioneer settler to the area.

"Now Andrew, let's not jump to conclusions jest yet. We'll talk about this outside. I got a load of taters and squash to trade before dark." J.L. wanted to defuse everyone's feelings before the rowdy bunch showed up. Leann was bull headed and ready for battle and he knew it! Everyone moved outside to the wagon load of produce and Big caught up with Job at the sheriff's office.

Sheriff Griggs had noticed the locals gathering at the store and met Job and Big on the front stoop of the building.

"Howdy men!" the sheriff said as he shook their hands.

Job got down to business and handed the letter from the sheriff in Nacogdoches to Griggs.

"Job Irvin and Big Miller, we brought a bag of mail down from Nacogdoches for the land office." Job stated their business in Burkeville.

"Well I declare, through Scrappin' Valley and in record time! 'Ol Cooter Simmons will be happy 'bout this. He's the town hall clerk." The sheriff's pleasure showed in his smile.

"I'll git you a receipt and meet you at the store." Griggs offered.

Job and Big walked back to Rackley's wagon to watch as folks scrambled to purchase the new potatoes and squash.

The excitement died down some as three men walked across the road from a rooming house. Job recognized the loud mouth fellow and positioned himself for what was to come. Big sensed Job's displeasure and followed his gaze to the three men. Sid herd had taken the bucket from the water boy.

Loud mouth started in right away, "I'll be, if it ain't the high steppin' Injun litterin' our streets agin'!" Sid Herd spouted off and stopped within arms reach of Job.

Sid Herd was what people called a "river rat". He lived northeast of town in what he called a fish camp. No one knew the exact location and no one cared to know. His ready cash meant he dealt in stolen goods and b-die whiskey. The two men with him were drifters that Sheriff Jacks had run out of town before for loitering and eye balling the ladies.

Job had already figured the odds and decided on his next move but wanted to avoid trouble if possible. These men were bullies and bluffers and had no idea they were stirring up a hornets nest. Job had been taught to "pursue peace" but if cornered to strike first and finish quick!

Sid Herd continued, directing his next sarcastic remark at Big, "I guess you one of them Injun lovin' Yankees?" Sid reached out to emphasize his point by laying a finger on Big's chest.

What happened next would be told a half dozen different ways for months to come. Sid's forefinger no sooner than touched Big's shirt when, Big brought the back of his huge right hand across the right side of Sid's face. The unexpected slap took Sid to his knees. Before he could even cry out, Big's number thirteen clod hopper caught him in the side of his neck. The kick rolled him flat of his back. Big was astraddle of the man with his fist drawn back as the man began to recover enough to beg for mercy. Big, layed down the law to Sid before he could speak.

"You chicken livered bum! Don't you ever lay a finger on me or insult a friend of mine again! You understand?!"

Big drew back to strike again when Sid pleaded, "Yeah mister! No offense Mister!" Sid rolled to his side and covered his bloody face.

No one, including Job, had been expecting such a quick and decisive response to Sid Herd's threat. Job had positioned himself to defend against the other two men but when they saw the awesome power and deadly intent of Big, they had craw fished away from the scene. Sheriff Griggs had witnessed the whole thing from his office window and smiling, he muttered to himself, "Made my job a lot easier!" He finished writing out the mail receipt and walked out to the crowd.

Big had backed away and Sid Herd half crawled and stumbled out of town toward the river. The crowd and street was quiet as a grave yard. Big turned as Sheriff Griggs approached and opened his mouth to defend his actions when the sheriff lifted his hands and said grinning, "I saw it, self defense, the man assaulted you!"

He handed Job the mail receipt and patted Big on the shoulder, saying, "You need a doctor or anything?"

"No sir" Big replied, "Just a drink of water and somethin' to eat." The water boy set his bucket of water on the ground and Big washed his bloody knuckles and sweat from his face.

Job handed the freckled face lad ten cents and spoke to Big. "I tried to warn you about that bucket of water!" as Job slapped Big on the back.

"The feller shouldn't have put his hand on me," Big replied seriously.

J.L spoke up, still amazed at the whirlwind event, "Boy, you sure cleaned his plow!"

Big had cooled down and nodding at Leann replied, "Miss Rackley, I apologize for such uncivilized behavior."

"You stop that frettin' Mr. Miller. There's no telling what no accounts like that would do if men like you didn't stop them." Leann said emphatically.

Big flushed red at her praise then turned to ready his horse for the trip back home.

J.L. spoke before the men could mount up to leave. "How 'bout you men stop by our place for the night? We'll butcher a couple of pullets and Leann might make some cat heads!"

He glanced at Leann for approval and she agreed with a nod and said, "You betcha'!

You'll be the first overnight guests we ever had!"

"You sure you got room?" Job asked.

"We got a couple extra nails we can hang you on!" Leann said laughing and the children all voiced their approval.

Job was encouraged by what he had seen and heard during the run in with Sid Herd. He knew the store would stay segregated but the local population was not as prejudiced as he had thought they would be. He knew the finger on his chest was not the only reason Big had reacted the way he did. Big Miller was a good man and a faithful friend. Job felt more than being indebted to him. He felt like family and for once in a long time, he was happy. He whistled a tune as he followed the Rackley's out of town and to their home.

CHAPTER 33

JUMP THE BROOM!

The days were getting longer and warmer in East Texas. There was no such thing as a lazy day on the Stanley farm. Just like the ant, folks were preparing for the winter months. The April showers were unpredictable and left everyone miserable in the lingering humidity.

Coop and Angie had taken up construction of the mud chimney on Job's cabin. Coop was a master carpenter and joiner so the foundation for the chimney was well underway. The back breaking labor was just what Angie needed to keep her mind off Job. They had been in Nacogdoches five days now with no word from Job or Big Miller. Every morning Angie would hang her pinafore next to the front door of the cabin, hoping to give Job a pleasant surprise when he came home.

Mrs. Miller had a prayer meeting every morning after the chores were done. This was a great support to all. Angie was expected to have a bible verse ready and her inspirationals were gladly received. She expected Job to ride into camp any moment. She had tried to imagine what it would be like to see him again. She often felt as though his spirit was touching hers and would pause to glance down the trail toward town.

Job and Big had been so impressed with the Rackley farm, they had stayed two nights. J.L had cleared twenty acres of bottom land and planted corn, cotton and tobacco. His property bordered the wilderness area of no man's land. There was land to be claimed so Job and Big rode out to scout the area. The rich soil, timber and wildlife was everything a pioneer could ask for in life. Big and Job were already dreaming and making plans to make another trip into the area again real soon.

The two nights of rest and good food had revived their spirits so Job and Big bid the Rackley's farewell. J.L. had given each man vegetable seeds and Leann fixed them a poke lunch for their trip. The children followed the two men to the edge of their field waving and asking for candy on their return trip.

Their plan was to ride hard for the next two days and hoped to get home by Friday evening. Job paid more attention to the flora and fauna on the trail. East Texas reminded him of Georgia. Poke salad, muscadines, possum grapes, huckleberries and may apple were abundant. The deer had worn trails through the creek bottoms. He and Big added more tree markings as they traveled. The frequent slashes on the tree trunks would allow a rider to travel at night if needed.

The men felt safe with a fire at night. They enjoyed Leann's lunch of cornbread and muscadine jelly. Job enjoyed raw squash with salt and Big made a face and shook his head no when offered a portion.

"You must have an iron stomach," Big remarked. "I'd have the walking farts all day if I ate like you!" he said with a chuckle.

"It keeps me light on my feet!" Job replied with a laugh out loud.

Friday at noon just an hour's ride from Nacogdoches, Job shot a nice spike buck deer. They field dressed it, anticipating fried back strap and Mrs. Miller's cat head biscuits for supper.

The ride home took them by the blacksmith shop in Nacogdoches. Spike seemed more glad than usual to see them.

"We got mail for you!" Spike said with a grin as the men dismounted and shook hands.

"Water your mounts and I'll close up here and ride home with you." Spike said and walked away. He slipped next door to the feed and tack room where Tater Smith sat oiling harnesses.

"Tater, head out to my place and tell the folks that Big and Job are headed that way, now run!" He ordered the boy, tossing him a two bit piece.

Tater lit out in a trot and Spike began closing shop with a big grin on his face. Big and Job noticed the smug grin as Spike met them at the water trough.

"Boy, you grinnin' like a new daddy!" Big remarked, hoping for a reason in reply.

"Tomorrow's payday and I got a raise!" Spike said, stretching the truth a little bit. They rode by the sheriff's office and dropped the mail receipt off then the men headed home while listening to Spike report on the local gossip.

Angie was cleaning up after a late lunch when Tater Smith came trotting into camp. He was big eyed and breathless as he relayed the message from Spike.

"Miss Angie, Spike said to tell ye Big Miller and Job is back and headed home right now!" The lad sat down and Angie brought him a dipper of cool water.

"Did you see them?" Angie asked anxiously.

"Yes Mam they was waterin' their mounts and fixin' to head this way!" Tater replied, finishing off two dippers of water.

Coop had heard the news and instructed Angie, "Honey, you go freshen up!" He grinned at Angie, noticing the glow on her face and the tears in her eyes. He waved Tater goodbye and walked to the Miller cabin to report the good news.

The riders were laughing and cutting up as they rode onto the Stanley farm. Big and Job noticed the extra wagon next to Job's cabin. They thought nothing of it for Mr. Stanley was always accommodating travelers that patronized his shop. Something was a little odd about Job's cabin but he couldn't make it out just yet.

Spike dropped back catching Big's eye and winked at him nodding in the direction of Job's cabin. "Angie!" he whispered, fashioning the word with his mouth hoping Big could read his lips.

"Looks like we got compnee'," Big spoke excitedly, grinning at Spike.

Job never caught the drift between the two men. He was a hundred yards from his cabin when he saw what looked like a poster hanging beside his front door. The shadows from the red oaks concealed the object until Job was a stones throw away. Job suddenly reined in Red and just sat staring at the object beside the door. He recognized the object as the pinafore he had bought for Angie but what swept over his spirit left him unable to speak. Big and Spike had dropped back to enjoy the moment.

Big spoke first, "Spike I think it's Job that's got compnee'!"

Spike couldn't contain himself any longer.

"That's right, and she's a beauty!" he reported excitedly grinning at Job who had never moved a muscle or stopped staring at the pinafore.

"Angie!" the almost audible name slipped from his lips and he glanced at Spike. Spike shook his head up and down grinning widely.

There was no movement in the camp when suddenly Angie stepped through the front door of Job's cabin into the light. Her auburn hair shone brightly in the sunlight. Coop followed behind her and stood grinning at Job.

Job swung down from the saddle and dumbfounded he took a step toward Angie. Her face was now wet with tears and she broke into a run and cried his name, "Job!"

The months of hardship, loneliness and heartache found complete release and Job shouted, "Angie!" as he ran to reach her.

Hot tears coursed down his face as they embraced and whispered each others name. Every eye in the camp was wet with tears. Mrs. Miller was weeping out loud and waving her apron in celebration. The children suddenly understood the occasion and began clapping and laughing. Red the mule began braying, sensing the excitement and being in familiar territory again.

The deer had been cleaned and a supper of back strap and biscuits had been served before dark. Angie was of no help to the ladies for Job would not let go of her hand or let her out of his sight. He hugged Coop and asked if he could call him Pop.

Mrs. Miller was thoroughly enjoying the romantic evening between Job and Angie and finally made the remark, "Look's like somebody's gonna be jumping the broom pretty quick!" Everyone laughed and joked about her declaration but Job and Angie were proposing marriage with every smile and touch.

Job had been making his plans to propose to Angie for weeks. He had the spot picked out down by the creek where he often rested among the shade of the maple trees. He would ask for permission from Ely and propose Saturday evening. The candles burned late that night in Job's cabin. Ellen's death was still a very sensitive issue and Job wept with Angie and Coop as they shared their story.

Saturday morning was a beehive of activity as everyone caught up on their chores. It was market day in Nacogdoches and after dinner everyone would go to town to enjoy payday and buy groceries and dry goods. Job had got Coop alone long enough to ask for Angie's hand in marriage. Coop led him on for a while and then said he was delighted with the decision. Job planned to tarry behind with Angie then catch up with everyone later in town.

The children had already clued Angie in on Job's favorite get away spot but she concealed the fact as he asked her to take a walk to the creek alone.

"You sure put me on the spot Job Irvin, having me to choose between sightseeing in town or taking a walk to the creek!" Angie said, poking fun at Job to lighten the mood.

"Ah! I just need to show you the best place to wash my clothes in the future." Job ribbed her right back with a grin.

Angie blushed red and tears filled her eyes studying Job's face as he led her to his favorite shady spot. He gathered her hands into his and gazed into her eyes adoringly as he spoke.

"Angie Cooper, I would like to court you properly and allow you time to settle in here but things move fast and furious out here. I believe in making hay while the sun's shining and there's a lot to do before winter." Job rambled on hoping for the proper words to make his point.

Angie was amused at his anxiety so as she placed one hand over his lips, she spoke, "Job Irvin, I love you. You can rest in that fact. Love has found a way in our lives. Now, speak your heart!" with that said, she took her hand away and smiled into his face.

Job placed a hand on each side of her lovely face and replied, "Angie Cooper, I love you! You are my soul mate. I want to spend the rest of my life with you and your Daddy agrees!" Job smiled searching her face for assurance and finally blurted out, "Will you marry me?"

Angie smiled as tears coursed down her cheeks and replied softly, "Yes, yes, yes, yes!" She never got another word out as Job pressed his lips into hers. He had not kissed her since the cold morning in Alabama months ago. The struggles, hardships and heartaches melted away as they embraced in the shade on the creek bank.

Their radiant faces gave their secret away as Job and Angie arrived in Nacogdoches later that evening. Everyone was gathered at Stanley's blacksmith shop as the two rode up. Mrs. Miller could read Angie's face and was all teary eyed waiting for the news. Job didn't know exactly what or how to break the news so he spoke first.

"Folks, I got Mr. Cooper's permission and Angie has accepted my proposal of marriage. Now, I need to get word to the preacher!"

Everyone laughed at the blunt announcement and the joy of the two spread quickly.

"I knew it was time to jump the broom, I told ya'll!" Mrs. Miller boasted and ran to hug Angie.

"I'd like to help you with your dress!" she offered and Angie agreed crying and laughing at the same time.

Coop sighed with relief as he hugged Job and said, "I'm happy and I know Ellen is happy now."

The wedding was planned for a month later to make time to finish Job's cabin. A wedding was a holiday on the frontier and everybody was invited. The ceremony took place on a Sunday morning after morning worship and a big dinner on the ground followed. Angie wore a simple cotton dress that her and Mrs. Miller put together, along with the pinafore Job gave her when they first met.

Job had never known such joy and happiness that he and Angie shared together. His reputation in leather craft kept him busy and Coop had a vegetable garden producing. There was not enough hours in a day to keep up.

Big and Job discussed the bountiful land down south next to the Rackley's and began to plan a trip to get the lay of the land. Even though it was dangerous, Job planned to take Angie along to meet the Rackleys and let her get a feel of the area.

He was happy for the time being but felt a stirring, a calling to the south. It was not a gamble but a fact that gripped his spirit. There was more for him and Angie in this territory. He was not boxed in and was a free man in Texas. Texas was now his home, his family's home. As he and Angie shared their dreams and plans, she would smile as he gazed into the distance and would conclude, "That's what I like about Texas!"

THE END